NEW YORK *RUN*

Jamie!
Visit my website at
www.SLTNEWYORKRUN.COM

Samuel Torcasio

Samuel L. Torcasio
© 2017

One

Sonny Thomas drove at a good clip on Route 81 Westbound traveling towards Binghamton, New York, not knowing who was chasing him. It was Autumn and the leaves had already begun to change their foliage.

Stephanie Martinorelli was sound asleep leaning her head on Sonny's shoulder. He thought to himself, what a difference a few days can make. The present situation had the two of them on the run from one of the most powerful figures in the United States, who happened to be her father-in-law. Alexander Martinorelli was a member of the ***Commission***, one of the elite political, business and criminal memberships in the United States. This group contained only 36 members who were placed strategically in various parts of the United States and controlled everything.

Due to some negligence, and, or carelessness on the part of Michael Martinorelli, the husband of Stephanie, and the son of Alexander, Stephanie was able to take possession of **Twelve Discs'** that contained every facet of the Martinorelli empire, including their payroll. These discs' had judges, senators, police officials, and prominent business people throughout the United States on the Martinorelli payroll. After perusing the discs', Stephanie knew that if her husband or father-in-law knew that she gained access to or had any knowledge of the contents of the discs' her life would be in jeopardy. Now, on the run with the assistance of Sonny Thomas they planned to make a New York Run from the Martinorelli Empire, until they could get the discs to the proper authority. At this point the primary focus was on survival until this could be accomplished.

It was only two days earlier when Sonny Thomas woke up later than usual as a result of too much indulgence at the previous evening's New York State Bar Association meeting.

Sonny Thomas was thirty-two years old and in excellent physical condition. He was 6'2 and weighed 215 pounds. He swam three times a week. He took great pride in staying in good shape.

He rushed and showered then sped to work. Even though Sonny was a licensed attorney, his career focus had been in the investigation field. While the theory of law fascinated him, the practice of law never appealed to him. In particular, he did not appreciate personal injury attorneys and their lottery mentality. He believed that an attorney should be a counselor to the general public and assist them at critical times in their lives. The focus of the majority of today's lawyer's was primarily on money and being a counselor was secondary.

Investigation was his passion. He utilized his law background often in conducting a myriad of investigations all over the State Of New York. Sonny Thomas and Associates conducted investigation and other services for corporations, law firms, insurance companies, and private clients. At times he would work on missing persons and intermittently with the FBI. Originally from Western New York, he serviced most of the state.

After graduating from Law School and a brief stint of general law practice, Sonny opened up his own business and from the start it was moderately successful.

Sonny arrived at his office at 10:00 AM, almost an hour later than usual. As he walked in the office he observed an attractive strawberry blonde who closely resembled his brief Law School relationship, Stephanie Smith.

Ashley, Sonny's administrative assistant, greeted her boss,

"Good Morning Sonny."

"Good Morning Ashley."

"There is a Ms. Sarah Dempsey waiting to speak to you."

"OK, I'll be ready in a second."

"Would you like some coffee? I just brewed it."

"Of course, you can bring Ms. Dempsey in."

Sonny sat behind his desk and looked at Sarah Dempsey. The resemblance with Stephanie was incredible. Sonny's heart beat a half second faster when he thought of Stephanie, which was more often than he wanted to admit to himself.

"Stephanie showed me pictures of you two, but in person the resemblance is incredible."

"Yeah, we have fooled a lot of people over the years."

"Ms. Dempsey, what can I help you with?"

Sarah Dempsey just started to cry. Sonny walked over and handed her a tissue.

"Mr. Thomas, you have to help me. You are the only one that can."

"What, what is it?"

"Stephanie is missing. When she spoke about you I could tell there was something special about the relationship you two had in Law School. She told me about the last week just before graduation. I am very scared because I feel her life is in danger."

Sonny immediately thought of the last week he had with Stephanie. His heart began to beat a little faster.

"Ms. Dempsey, how long has Stephanie been missing?"

"Two days."

"She had mentioned to me that if she ever were to go missing to contact you given your reputation in the community and the fact that you know her. She was adamant and said that you would be the only one able to find her."

"Why would she be missing? Any thoughts?"

"There is something about that family, the Martinorelli's, that I just don't trust. They have so much money that they have to be just as powerful and probably have many criminal ties. Shortly after their marriage Stephanie would call me crying about how she had made the biggest mistake of her life and could do nothing about it. When I would ask her what it was she would just say it was too late. Can you please find my sister? I have a feeling her life is in danger."

Sonny paced the room a little, looked outside and saw an unfamiliar black limousine parked directly across the street. He grabbed his cup of coffee and sat next to Stephanie's twin.

"When was the last time you spoke with Stephanie?"

"Two days ago. We have talked every day our entire lives Mr. Thomas other than the last two. I am really scared."

Sarah, again began to softly cry. Sonny grabbed some more Kleenex and wiped her wet eyes.

"I will get right on it, Sarah. Stephanie and I were pretty close in Law School. Even though it has been a couple of years I still think about her. She really broke my heart. If she is in trouble I have to try and help her. As for you, I want you to get out of town because if that family is as powerful as you think you will be a top priority for them. We cannot risk giving them the opportunity to use you to get to Stephanie. Give all your information to Ashley and I will get in touch with you as soon as I find something out."

"Thank you, Mr. Thomas."

Sarah got up and hugged Sonny. He hugged her back.

"I don't want you leaving yet. I will make arrangements to have you brought to your house with security. I'll take care of your car also. Pack as quick as you can and text Ashley where you are ASAP. Again, I will get in touch with you as soon as I can."

Two

It was the final year of Law School. The study group of Stephanie Smith, Louis Charles and Sonny Thomas were eager to graduate and start practicing law after the New York State Bar exam that July.

The study group was very close. They started the study group after they met at a party in the beginning of their first year. They seemed to be regular down to earth people unlike some of the other first year Law students. The other Law students were a little pompous and overall condescending.

First year classes included: Real Property, Contracts, Torts, Constitutional Law, Criminal law, Civil Procedure, Legal Research and Writing and Evidence. The group met three nights a week and they shared each others outlines and became close friends very fast. The three ate together, went to happy hours together, and genuinely enjoyed each others company.

During the first trimester of the first year, Sonny asked Stephanie out every single day. He totally fell for her immediately. Stephanie turned him down every day because she was loyal to her fiance, Michael Martinorelli. The two mutually had a hidden crush on one another. Stephanie was 5 '9 and weighed 135 pounds and was a part time model when she was in College. She was stunningly beautiful with the prettiest green eyes. She was on the synchronized swimming team in High School and regularly swam to stay in shape.

Sonny accepted her denials, but deep down he knew that they were right for each other. Stephanie kept her loyalty to Michael, but she was as much infatuated with Sonny as he was with her. To Sonny, Stephanie was perfect. Beautiful, athletic, intelligent, and even a black belt. Most of all, she was a caring friend. The most giving person he had ever met. He would continue to be patient and wait.

Stephanie came from an impoverished background. Her father died when Stephanie and her twin sister, Sarah, were in the eighth grade. It was just Sarah and Stephanie. Her mother was never the same after she lost her husband at such a young age. Mrs. Smith had a rough childhood and it affected her relationship with the twins. After coming from this background, Stephanie's primary focus was on monetary success. She loved the Law and her desire was to become a successful trial attorney. She excelled academically and worked hard at everything she did.

During Christmas break of their second year of Law School, Stephanie decided to stay on campus. When Sonny heard this he changed his Christmas plans and stayed on campus also. Stephanie was getting angry with Michael and the Martinorelli family because of their suffocating possessiveness. The phone calls on a regular basis and his demand that she be at his side 24/7 was getting to her. She thought often about calling off the wedding, but he would apologize and things would be better for a short while and then return back to normal.

Sonny and Stephanie spent every day together. This time, however, Sonny never made a romantic advance on Stephanie. He thought she had turned him down enough, and his pride would not let him do it again. Though deep down, he really wanted to.

Stephanie, on the other hand, was waiting for a romantic advance now, but it never materialized. She wanted him now. Nothing romantic happened. She wanted to make an advance on Sonny, but she would chicken out and then think of her upcoming wedding.

The two became better friends and really enjoyed the Christmas break together. One evening before the trimester was to begin Stephanie walked over to Sonny's to tell him how she really felt about him, but at the last minute she changed her mind and went home. Alone.

After the trimester resumed, the two continued to meet at their study group with Louis, but the emotions of both had changed. All this time Sonny had feelings for Stephanie, but he had an issue with her past pattern of saying no to him. Nevertheless, he still wanted to be with her.

Stephanie wondered why Sonny had not made any advances on her during the Christmas break. She thought well maybe it has to be my move. I did turn him down a lot she thought.

Sonny always felt in his heart that Stephanie and he would eventually become an item; however, it was her turn to make the romantic advance.

During the final week of their third year subsequent to finals, there were a lot of parties. The exaltation of completing the rigorous three years of Law School was an exciting time for the soon to be Law graduates.

One evening, Sonny arrived at a party alone as he was running late finishing up a final paper that was overdue. He walked in and observed Stephanie across the room. His heart always beat a little faster when he first saw her. She was talking to another third year who clearly, at least to Sonny, was hitting on her. Sonny observed this and was getting angry because Stephanie appeared to enjoy this. Sonny turned around to leave the party as he could not imagine Stephanie with anyone, but himself.

Stephanie spotted Sonny leaving and maneuvered through the crowd and the loud music over to him. She grabbed his arm.

"Hey, where's the fire?"

"I'm a little tired. Haven't slept well lately. Going to have a night cap and go to bed."

"Sonny, this is the last party. We graduate Sunday. Don't you want to spend time with me?"

"I would, but your engaged."

Sonny looked at Stephanie. Stephanie looked back at Sonny, she saw a tear in his eye and she was consumed with affection for him. She at first hugged him and then kissed Sonny, romantically, who did not resist. Then Stephanie started crying and the two left the party together. Sonny's tears were because he knew Stephanie was going to be married soon and he could not stand it. Stephanie cried because her affection for Sonny could not be hidden anymore.

The two of them could not keep their hands off of each other, hugging, kissing, laughing all the way to Stephanie's apartment. They rushed into her apartment disrobing each other, and quickly were in bed.

The lovemaking between Sonny and Stephanie was magical. After the first episode, Stephanie just laid on top of Sonny looking into his eyes.

"If I had known this, I would have said yes two years ago."

"Better late than never," responded Sonny.

"I knew we would end up together, Steph."

Sonny, finally felt things were going his way with Stephanie. The two did not speak much, but they didn't have to. Sonny held Stephanie like they were one. Afraid that if he let her go that she would disappear and this would all have been only a dream. After several episodes they fell asleep in each others arms.

The next afternoon Sonny awoke with Stephanie on top of him kissing his face repeatedly. He reached for her and they proceeded, again, to make love throughout the afternoon. While Sonny thought about telling Stephanie how he felt, he was worried how she would react. He did not want to change anything at this point. Because of the past rejections, he would have to hear it from her first.

Stephanie knew how she felt about Sonny, but, she was going to get married in a couple of months. For the time being all she wanted was Sonny.

"Steph…I have to…"

"No, Sonny. Let's not talk now."

He held onto her and they, again, fell asleep in each others arms.

The following morning, a Saturday, a day before the graduation ceremony, they ate breakfast together. Sonny made arrangements for the two to get a room, Monday, at the local Crown Plaza. After the graduation ceremony, Monday would be a great relaxing time for the two of them. The room number 3107 even matched each others birthday so it appeared as if it was meant to be. Stephanie 10/31 and Sonny 12/7.

On Monday evening, Sonny and Stephanie slow danced together, ate dinner, and made love until they fell asleep in each others arms, again. It was the happiest time in Sonny and Stephanie's life. Their conversations were intelligent but concise until they were back in bed, *again.* *They* made the perfect couple.

The following morning Sonny awoke, but he was alone. Stephanie had left. He noticed a piece of paper on one of the chairs. He got up, grabbed his bath robe and ran to the chair. He read the note.

Dearest Sonny:

I hate to leave this way, but I am so confused. I could not say Goodbye to you. My time with you felt so right. I loved every minute of it. Please, never change. Maybe, one day, our paths will cross in the future, but by continuing this it is not fair to either of us. I do not want to continue hurting you by doing this anymore. I am going to be married soon. I am sorry for leaving a note like this. I will never forget you, or our time together.

Love always,

Stephanie

Sonny put the note down. He knew his time with Stephanie was temporary. He just hoped it was forever. It was inevitable that it would end. Sonny felt a feeling he never felt before – his heart ached, he physically felt his heart breaking in two.

Three

After Sonny met with Sarah Dempsey and made all the necessary arrangements he said goodbye to her. Based on her observation the Martinorelli family was very powerful, wealthy, and most likely criminal which is why she did not trust them. She, specifically, did not like the possessiveness that Michael Martinorelli demonstrated on her sister. It was a common complaint from Stephanie. Sonny had a pretty good idea where Stephanie was located.

Sonny drove part of the way to locate Stephanie. After thinking about her whereabouts he *knew* where she was. After locking his car he took the subway a few miles. Finally, he walked the last five blocks just in case he was being followed. He did not like the fact that when Sarah was at his office there was a mysterious black limousine parked across the street from his office. He was pretty certain that Stephanie was there based on what her sister told him.

It had been a couple of years since they graduated from Law school. His heart was beating a little quicker as he thought of Stephanie. He arrived at the Crown Plaza and took the elevator to the third floor. He knocked on the door at room 3017. Stephanie opened the door and burst into tears when she saw Sonny. She embraced Sonny very tightly. Sonny returned the hug. She looked at him and just smiled. Then her smile vanished.

"Do you think you were followed?"

"I don't think so. I drove part of the way, parked in a garage and took the subway to about five blocks away. Then I walked the rest of the way. Remember what I do for a living."

Stephanie smiled again. To Sonny she had not changed one bit.

They reluctantly let go of each other and sat on the edge of the king bed. Stephanie, as beautiful as Sonny could remember, was dressed in silk pajamas and a silk bathrobe.

"So let's start at the beginning. Why are you running from your husband's family?"

"Sonny, it's difficult to explain. The wedding and the honeymoon were okay, but there was something missing in our relationship."

"I see. Why did you marry him? You knew how much I loved you."

"Michael became very possessive shortly after we were married, more so than he already was. I felt that he was hiding something from me. I just did not know what. I was pretty certain that he was being unfaithful to me, but I could never substantiate it."

"I am sorry to hear that, Stephanie."

"I really don't think Michael loves me. He loves the idea of being married to someone like me, I guess. I really don't know."

Sonny got up and walked to the door and checked the peephole. He came back and sat next to Stephanie. The thoughts in his head were consumed with Stephanie and their last week in Law School. It was difficult to think about anything else.

"Sonny, my immediate dilemma is that I know everything there is to know about the Martinorelli family."

Sonny got up and walked over to pour himself a cup of coffee. He sat next to Stephanie his heart beating fast now.

"What can you tell me about Michael's family? I know of the Martinorelli family, their National Law Firm and some of their businesses, but nothing illegal."

"Sonny, Alexander Martinorelli runs one of the top criminal and powerful empires in the eastern portion of the United States. He is a board member of the *Commission*, an elite organization that controls most political business and criminal activities in the entire United States. He has circumvented any bad publicity or the fact that his empire includes criminal activities because he is a successful, powerful lawyer throughout the nation. His law firm touches a lot of businesses throughout the country. Again, he is a long time board member of the ***Commission***."

Sonny continued drinking his coffee. He would have to investigate this ***Commission***. He had contacts at the District Attorney's office. Louie Charles.

Stephanie got up and paced the room. She could not believe how good Sonny looked. She felt guilty about the letter she had left a couple of years ago. Now everything had changed. She needed Sonny to assist her and get out of this predicament she was in. She sat next to Sonny on the King bed. She started to cry again.

"Thank you so much for coming Sonny. There must be someway we can get these discs' to the FBI. I did not know any of the criminal part of his family until I discovered the discs, Sonny. You have to believe me. My Father-in-law and Husband now know that I have all of the critical information about all of their businesses, criminal and legitimate. Now that I ran with the discs, I feel they would rather kill me than risk a chance that I would talk to any authorities like the FBI."

Sonny got up and walked around the room. Stephanie also got up and stood in front of Sonny.

"Sonny, you are the only person in the world I could turn to."

"Well?" asked Stephanie.

"Can you help me get these discs' to the FBI so the Martinorelli empire finally gets justice?"

Stephanie began to gently sob, again. Sonny's heart was beating. He walked over to her and hugged her. Sonny looked at Stephanie, his emotions were running wild. He had a relationship with Stephanie, but it ended abruptly. He never forgot her; however, and he was never over her either. Assisting her now would jeopardize his career, and perhaps, his life. He could not say no to her regardless of the danger he would immediately inherit.

He would have to obtain as much information on Alexander Martinorelli and obtain it fast. While Sonny had heard of Alexander Martinorelli, none of it concerned any criminal element. Even if he were to get Stephanie out of New York City...then what? He knew the intelligent decision would be to stay away. His heart told him otherwise. Besides, who else can help her now.

"Sure, Stephanie I'll try to help you, but I have to investigate the Martinorelli Family and their empire first."

"Wait."

Stephanie ran and grabbed the discs. She handed Sonny all twelve of them.

"Review these discs. They will convey to you the criminal power that Alexander Martinorelli has, and how it touches political, business and criminal dimensions."

"OK. I'll review them and devise a getaway plan for us to initially get out of New York. You stay here for now. Are you sure that no one else knows where you are?"

"No one, but you."

"Let me go to my office, make some phone calls and review these discs. I will be back here tonight."

Stephanie rushed over to Sonny.

"Oh, thank you, Sonny. I knew I could count on you."

Stephanie kissed Sonny on the lips followed by a lengthy hug.

"Well, let's just say I enjoy your company."

Stephanie smiled. She had to say something about the two of them.

"Sonny, these last couple of years, have you thought about me?"

"I have. What about you?"

"I have too."

Sonny kissed Stephanie on the forehead and left, his heart, again, beating a step and a half faster than normal. He realized that his feelings for her had never changed.

Four

Michael Martinorelli paced back and forth. His father sat behind his desk looking at his son. How could his own son permit his wife to obtain all the family business records and now disappear. It has been two days since Stephanie Martinorelli has been missing. Alexander stood up and addressed his son. It was only the two of them in the office.

"Michael, you do realize the problem Stephanie poses for our family don't you?"

"Pop, I do, but isn't there any other option?"

"No. At this point she knows our contacts, our affiliations, all of our business, and, finally, the politicians on our payroll. There is no other option. I am sorry, but your inattentiveness permitted Stephanie to go somewhere she should not have gone. She has possession of critical information that could ruin us all."

Alexander got up and walked to Michael. He patted his son on the back. Alexander was angry, but he envisioned getting the discs back quickly and his business would return to normal

"Michael, I have worked my entire life to build the perfect impenetrable organization. Those discs could ruin the family along with many powerful and influential people. We must get those discs immediately."

Alexander Martinorelli walked over to the window and daydreamed about the past. For over 40 years he ran his many businesses without a hiccup. Now his own daughter-in-law could end it all. He thought about the beginning.

Alexander Martinorelli was an exceptional man. Born after World War II he was raised an Italian Catholic. His father ran a local butcher shop in the heart of Little Italy, New York. His father also was one of New York's biggest bookies under the local Fabruguzzio family. His mother was a typical Italian Catholic mother who went to church every morning. She was an exceptional cook. He also had a younger sister, Angela, whom he revered. Leukemia took Angela at age 10. Alexander Martinorelli was a big family man and always stressed in later years that only family can really be trusted.

He excelled in school which always came easy to him. Eventually, he excelled in the streets. Alexander observed firsthand how his father ran a successful legitimate business, but was as equally intrigued how the illegal business, booking, actually financed his family. The number of people who would bet their paycheck on numbers seemed totally foreign to what young Alexander envisioned later when he would become an adult.

Alexander met and enjoyed the company of underworld figures of New York. In particular, young Alexander looked up to one of the families of New York that ran their family like a corporation. This family seemed to have a piece of many different legitimate businesses along with their criminal empire. This intrigued Alexander.

The present Don, or head of the family, had previously murdered the former Don of the family. While seemingly ruthless that is the way it worked then. He then became the new Don and took over the family business himself. How this act of murder benefited the actual murderer remained with Alex for a lifetime.

At a young age as Alexander was sweeping up in the back of the butcher shop where most of the booking was taking place, he overheard a conversation that would change his future. Robby Lucia, Steve Maglio, Paulie Cerrone and the Don, Pete Fabruguzzio, were in a heated discussion.

"Pete if we don't get more involved in this drug trafficking, the other families will get stronger and eventually wipe us out. We won't be able to match the money they will make," remarked Robby.

Steve nodded in agreement, followed shortly by Paulie. Robby added,

"Pete, don't you see where this is leading?"

Pete Fabruguzzio was the head of the family. While soft spoken, he lived on the streets virtually his entire life. He stood up and walked around the table. He looked at his three associates.

"Look, I agree that narcotics is good business. Much profit, but much risk. It may ruin us if not handled correctly. With the Narcotics Control Act now in effect, the Feds would target families that dealt in drugs."

Young Alexander listened as Pete Fabruguzzio continued:

"As a family, we have to change with the times. We have to insulate ourselves from any possible weak links. With narcotics as a major source of revenue, we risk having an associate of ours pinched and serve twenty to thirty years. Now we can buy silence for three to five years, but with twenty to thirty years we will be ratted out by our own associate's. I agree that we should pursue narcotics, but on a limited scale thereby limiting risk. There is more than ample opportunity to make revenue in the legitimate world. Regardless of what the FBI says, our best weapon is and always will be secrecy.

Robby, Steve and Paulie continued to badger back and forth, but Pete Fabruguzzio had spoken. What Pete did not realize was how this conversation affected young Alexander Martinorelli.

Throughout his school years, Alexander Martinorelli excelled academically. He graduated at the top of his class in High School. He then graduated from working at his father's butcher shop to working directly for Pete Fabruguzzio. He looked up to Pete, but always wanted to be the Don with a little different style than Pete Fabruguzzio.

Pete liked Alexander and on an almost daily basis explained the day to day operations of running his family. Alexander attended horse races and gambling joints with the made members of the Fabruguzzio family. While with them on a daily basis, he could not understand how most of them blew all their money. At age eighteen, Alexander was investing his score money and growing it exponentially. He was always lending money to associates who rarely, if ever, paid him back.

After graduating college, again, at the top of the class, Alexander was accepted into Harvard Law School. He graduated from Harvard Law School, again, at the top of his class. He felt that he was ready to pursue the legal world, the business world of Wall Street, and his own personal ambitions of running his own family.

While Alexander was educated at the finest academic institutions in the world, he kept a pulse on the underworld criminals that controlled as much through their legitimate business interests as they did through their criminal element.

Alexander went out of his way to follow some of the Don's, or the head of families, that were still able to control as much legitimate business and still run it like a corporation.

One particular Don controlled the New York airports, private garbage disposals throughout New York, waterfront businesses in New York, securities market fraud on Wall Street, trucking, loan sharking and heroin distribution. This was an empire Alexander Martinorelli wanted to emulate. He later learned that this particular Don owned the garment district in New York. It was estimated that seventy percent of all clothing sold in the United States came from that seven block area in lower Manhattan. Alexander could not wait to get in on the action. Right around then Alexander started his Law practice. Around this time the Rico Statutes were putting more made men in federal prison than ever before. The Rico Statutes permitted the FBI and District Attorney's to arrest and prosecute the head of any family whose "member" was found guilty of any crime. Any family unprepared would pay the consequences and lose everything.

A parade of bosses went to trial and many died in prison. Las Vegas was immersed with made families throughout the country. They had been there ever since Bugsy Siegel envisioned a world class entertainment center in the middle of the Nevada desert. While he never lived to see it, Las Vegas grew and grew and for awhile families from New York, Chicago, Kansas City and Los Angeles were there skimming off their own casinos and getting away with it. It eventually came to and end.

After running the casino's for decades the different families from all over the United States eventually were moved out and replaced by corporations, which made Las Vegas even more popular and more lucrative. While the families were still there it was on a more limited basis that included primarily strip clubs and small gambling joints.

As Pete Fabruguzzio had predicted years earlier, families lost button men, under bosses and any associate who was pinched. These former family members either went to prison or became part of the Witness Protection Program by ratting out other made members by testifying against them. The families became weaker with each arrest and/or losing an associate to this Witness Protection Program.

Alexander Martinorelli saw it coming and while still part of the Fabruguzzio family, his focus was on his new Law practice. He did not frown on these times as he envisioned it as a future opportunity to take over. He would devise a family that was impenetrable from the FBI or any other police agency. Opposing families would not be strong enough to compete with his family. There was one obstacle, however, Pete Fabruguzzio.

Even at this young age, Alexander was cunning. His most formidable weapon he would utilize in his climb to power was not muscle, but brains. Alexander had "*Furberia*" an Italian word meaning a wary cleverness, a slyness, the astuteness of an individual who evaluates and studies all of the angles before he makes a final decision. That was Alexander.

Five

Sonny arrived back at his office early afternoon. Ashley was gone to lunch. He retrieved his mail and began looking through it. There was a knock on the door. Then the door opened and two rather large men of Italian descent dressed in black double breasted pin stripe suits walked into Sonny's office. Sonny pushed the envelope with the **Twelve Discs** under his desk.

"Can I help you gentlemen?"

"Yeah, you can. We heard through the grapevine that the twin sister of Stephanie Martinorelli was here this morning."

Sonny immediately thought of the unknown black limousine parked across the street from his office earlier. He looked out the window and the same black limousine was there.

"I can't discuss with you any conversation I had with a prospective client. What exactly do you gentlemen want?"

"Look Mr. Thomas, my Boss would greatly appreciate it if you would respect his request to not communicate with Stephanie Martinorelli. He would consider it a great favor and would be able to quadruple the amount of business you currently have. He knows you are a respected man in the community. Of course he does also offer other financial compensation for this request."

The large man tossed a large envelope full of 100 dollar bills on Sonny's desk with several intentionally falling out. Sonny figured at least $100,000 was there do to the size of the 8 by 11 large envelope. He stood up and paused. He had to take a stand or these guys would eat him alive. He walked directly in front of both men.

"Look gentlemen, I cannot be bought. Whoever your Boss is tell him I cannot be bought. Bribes, cash mean nothing to me. I will communicate with whoever I wish. Now get the hell out of my office."

Sonny tossed the envelope full of 100 dollar bills back to the large man.

"Forget about it Mr. Thomas. Stephanie has something that does not belong to her. We have been advised to explain to you the ramifications of turning down the Boss. The Boss always wins. You help Stephanie and you jeopardize both of your lives and any one close to you."

The two men turned around and started to walk out of Sonny's office. Abruptly, the second large man picked up a lounge chair and threw it into the wall, breaking a few of Sonny's favorite pictures. The man turned to Sonny and just grinned.

Sonny's heart raced. What had he gotten himself into. After the two men left he proceeded to call his Law School buddy, Louie Charles, who was an Assistant District Attorney in the Bronx.

"Louie, it's me Sonny."

"Hey bud, what's up?"

"I have to meet with you as soon as possible. It's an emergency."

"No problem. Where?"

"I may be bugged."

"Let's meet at our usual hangout."

"30 minutes, okay."

"I'm on my way."

Sonny and Louie met at their Alma Mater in the Law School library. It was a joke, but it worked perfectly today. They went into a study room and viewed all **Twelve Discs** together. After the last disc was complete, Sonny turned off the computer and looked at Louie.

"Sonny, you and Stephanie are obviously very close friends of mine, dealing with a man with this much power is suicidal."

"I never said this would be easy."

"I am relatively new at the District Attorney's office, but I learned early on that Alexander Martinorelli is a big hitter and maybe the largest contributor to our office. Six figures a year is what I heard."

"Lou, I want you to be careful, but can you dig a little more into Alexander Martinorelli's background independent from the perspective of the DA's office. Based on what we both just observed, he would stop at nothing to get these discs back. The goons that visited me earlier were sent to give me a clear message. Do not get involved with Stephanie, or else."

"Let me go and investigate a little further into this guy. Like I said, he is like royalty at the DA's office."

"Lou, anything you get will be helpful. I plan on getting out of New York tomorrow night. My plan is eventually to get these discs to the FBI, but based on all his political connections I need as much information as possible."

"Will do."

Sonny left the library with the **Twelve Discs** and headed back to his office.

Six

The year was 1975 and the country was still getting over Vietnam and Watergate. Alexander Martinorelli was angry about all of the bad press the Don, Pete Fabruguzzio, was getting since his recent indictment as were other associates.

He had thought about it for a year or so now. While he respected Pete Fabruguzzio he was confident he could run a more impenetrable, flawless, affluent organization. Alexander had been catching the ear of the top men of Pete Fabruguzzio's family for months. He also was communicating with the members of the *Commission* without the knowledge of Pete Fabruguzzio. The Don's latest indictment for racketeering, fraud and extortion was the last straw. He would bring his entire family down including the rising star, Alexander Martinorelli, if something was not done. Alexander would, with the permission from the *Commission* and the family, end the reign of Pete Fabruguzzio.

It was late on a Friday night in the middle of January. The temperature was below zero and snowing lightly. They were a block away from Pete's office in the heart of downtown Manhattan. The two men, Alexander Martinorelli and Pete Fabruguzzio, walked alone down an alley in the center of

Manhattan. Pete was more nervous than Alexander ever recalled. He spoke constantly unlike his normal demeanor.

"No need to worry, Alex, with all my political connections, I will beat this rap and before you know it business will be back to normal. The *Commission* is 100 percent behind me."

"Positive, Pete?"

"Absolutely."

"Well, I don't think so Pete. I have been in contact with a lot of them. They are concerned. To be frank they are concerned that you will talk and rat them out."

"Alex, are you serious? They know I would never betray them. They would never abandon me. Not with all of the money I made them."

The two men walked before Pete finally said something. He stopped and looked at his protege.

"One day when this is all behind us, I want to talk to you about your future. In fact, someday I believe that you will be the Don and running my family."

"Thanks Pete, I appreciate that. I am, however, concerned."

"What do you mean, Alex?"

"Weakness breeds weakness, Pete. The FBI is winning because families don't have an adequate business plan to insulate ourselves from our own weaknesses."

"I am prepared, Alex. Once this indictment business is over, I'll have a sit down and arrange any and all future plans. We can even incorporate some of your ideas."

Alexander could not stand to hear any more weakness. He stopped and reached for his 45, and pointed it at his mentor. He knew this was the only answer.

"You're weak Pete. Eventually, you'll bring us all down."

Pete Fabruguzzio stopped, turned around and glared at the 45 being held by his protege pointed at his chest. All the time he spent with this rising star and he turns on me. Pete positioned himself directly across from Alexander.

"I am not weak, Alex."

He then reached for his own weapon. He did not make it. Alexander fired two shots into the heart of Pete Fabruguzzio. The third and final shot went into the forehead of the Don, killing him instantly.

Alexander did not shed a tear for his former mentor. Pete's own men were part of the assassination plot as were members of the *Commission*. Once Pete Fabruguzzio was under indictment, he was a risk not worth taking for the family. With the parade of wise guys talking to the FBI ratting our their own families then going to the witness protection program, there was no choice, but to end the reign of Pete Fabruguzzio.

Upon his death, there would have to be a successor to the role of head of the family. It would be Pete's choice. Alexander Martinorelli after several months of meetings was now the head of his new family at the ripe old age of twenty-nine years old.

Once the dead body of Pete Fabruguzzio was removed and thrown into the trunk of a black limousine, never to be found, she came out of the shadows. What she just witnessed could not be real. The tears flowed onto her cheeks. She did not know what to do. What would she do?

What would her children do? She witnessed Alexander Martinorelli murder crime boss, Pete Fabruguzzio, her husband. *She couldn't do anything.*

Seven

Alexander Martinorelli hated imperfection. Since he was appointed head of the family in 1975, forty plus years ago, he avoided mistakes that would threaten his empire. Through the years since the "disappearance" of Pete Fabruguzzio he had acquired ownership of casinos, construction companies, unions on a nationwide basis, garbage companies, banks, insurance companies, state lotteries and his own national law firm. This law firm was very successful, even though he was not involved in the day to day operations, he was chairman of the firm. His firms were located in New York, Newark, Chicago, Los Angeles, Las Vegas, Miami, Seattle and Houston.

This firm covered every aspect of law and was one of the largest in the United States. The firm practiced in all fields of law including: Personal Injury, Criminal Law, Estate Planning, Bankruptcy, Domestic Relations, Workers Compensation, and his favorite Corporation Law. It had been some time since Alexander actually practiced law personally, but he kept his license active.

Alexander acquired all these businesses by being clever, but remaining surreptitious as he exponentially built an empire that appeared to the average citizen as being 100 percent legitimate. He also controlled the criminal element, but this could never be traced to him. He was Alexander Martinorelli, lawyer, successful business man and owner of several charitable foundations. From the perspective of the average citizen he was a successful altruistic businessman who actively donated his time and money to a plethora of charities in the United States and Europe.

As a result of all of his business interests and criminal interest, he became a "member" of the *Commission.* This ultra-powerful organization included thirty-six of the most powerful families that literally ran the country. Unlike the 1930's commission which focused on the criminal element, this new commission focused more on the legitimate business interests, the white collar crimes which were more lucrative and safer. They still had their criminal interest and that also was lucrative, but the potential for both working together built an organization that had never been known to be as powerful in the United States. Other members included individuals who were at some point world bankers, federal reserve members, billionaires, politicians, members of the tri-lateral commission and finally members of the builderberg group. This group was easily the most powerful in contemporary times.

Alexander escaped the Rico Statutes because he guaranteed any member of his organization a prison term of five years or less were they to be pinched by a police agency. In the interim, the associate's family would be taken care of protection wise and financially during the prison term. Not a bad deal for both sides. This mutual deal prevented any of his associates partnering with the Federal Government as their future in the legitimate world was secure and lucrative.

Once the associate's prison term was over they would be set up in one of Alexander's legitimate businesses. This type of reciprocal agreement maintained his associate's loyalty. With the vast empire of business ownership throughout the United States it was impossible to connect Martinorelli with any of the myriad of companies that he owned. Corporate law guaranteed to conceal his real ownership of all these multi-million dollars companies, throughout the nation and Europe.

The only company he owned that could be traced with his own name was the Martinorelli Law firm. His overall payroll on a nationwide basis included, of course, his Law firm and all of the companies he owned. It also included nationwide, judges, politicians, police personnel, stock market associates and even members of the state department.

Alexander Martinorelli had always been one move ahead of everyone. Until now. He asked his secretary,

"Jordyn, can you please bring me some coffee, here?"

" Of course, Mr. Martinorelli."

Seated across from him were four very powerful, but now somewhat subdued gentlemen: New York Court of Appeals Judge, Alfred Rossi; Vice-President of Companion Insurance Company, Steven Modino; New York City Police Chief, Roger Fordrani; and, head of the Local Teamsters union, Anthony Amato.

"Let me explain to all of you, if she somehow is able to get those discs to the FBI, everyone here and beyond here will never be the same. The information on those discs will publicize names that will be investigated by the Feds. This will mean the end to a lot of lucrative business interests. These individuals will not be happy."

"Alex, don't worry, we'll find her," responded Police Chief, Roger Fordrani.

He was a local patrolman, a nine to fiver, before his gambling habit brought him to an associate of Alexander Martinorelli's, whom he owed over a hundred thousand dollars. After an arrangement was made Fordrani promptly rose in the rank and file of the police department. This was over ten years earlier. He was owned by Alexander.

"I have over one hundred patrolmen looking only for Stephanie Martinorelli. I am confident they will find her and bring her to you. I won't let you down."

Alexander walked around the huge conference table twice. He looked at the four men. He took a swig of his coffee then slammed it on his desk spilling most of it. This startled the four men.

"Either she disappears and I get my property back, or she is dead and I get my property back. I have no preference. If she gets away, Roger, you will personally have to answer for that. Understood?"

"I, I understand."

"Alex, we all recognize the position you are in. We all have to be patient. We must utilize all of our resources to ensure that the discs do not get to the FBI," interjected Court of Appeals Judge, Alfred Rossi.

"I agree," said Alexander.

Alexander walked to the window staring at the street below for what appeared to be several minutes. He turned to the four gentlemen.

"You have forty-eight hours to get her and those discs. Any questions?"

Steven Modino, the speckled almost feminine man blushed, while Anthony Amato signed loudly. In all the years that they worked with Alexander they had never seen him lose his temper like he just did. They were anxious to leave his office.

"Get out and find her, *NOW!*"

Alexander stood and stared at these powerful men as they exited the room. He was out of control thought these gentlemen as they left. This was not the Alex they knew all these years.

After they left, Alexander Martinorelli drank the rest of his coffee. He thought, all these years I had everything under control. The ***Commission*** will not be happy if this information is transferred to the FBI. What if this information is leaked to the press and internet. He thought he must prevent those discs from going to the FBI at any cost.

Eight

Sonny returned to his office. He quickly read his e-mails and texts. He followed up on a few phone calls. He briefly reviewed the new assignments.

"Ashley, call Lisa Taylor. I need her help with these new assignments."

Lisa Taylor was twenty-nine years old, a former police officer that retired at an early age after being successful in a sexual discrimination lawsuit against her former police precinct. Lisa was a brunette and stood 5 feet 9 inches. She was drop dead gorgeous. Lisa's background included an undergraduate degree in criminal justice. She had always wanted to be a police officer since she could remember.

Once Lisa finally finished at the academy, she learned very quickly how corrupt the precinct was. After being at the precinct for only a year, she refused to cooperate with her police colleagues. Her life was threatened and she was on the receiving end of many unwanted sexual advances. Subsequent to many discussions with those in charge and getting nowhere, she decided to sue the precinct. Fortunately, she won and was now a millionaire.

Lisa still worked because she became bored very easily. She opened her own private investigation company that specialized in the location of missing persons. When she was not traveling the world, Lisa assisted Sonny when he had an overflow of work. She enjoyed working with Sonny and she had a mad crush on him, but knew there was some one special in his past that he was not over.

Lisa met Sonny at an insurance investigation convention in Syracuse, New York a few years earlier. Sonny could not get over how beautiful Lisa was. Brief discussions lead to dinner and a mini romance that remained to this day. They were not a couple, but they occasionally took time off from work and would rendezvous a few times a year. Lisa confided to Sonny about her brief police career and her successful sexual discrimination lawsuit. Sonny begged Lisa to become his partner, but she refused and told Sonny she already had a company. She did tell him she would help him whenever she could.

"Sonny, I have Lisa on the phone."

"Hi Lisa, I need your help with some of my new assignments. Can you help me out?"

"Yes I can. I'm actually in between jobs so now is perfect for me."

"I have to leave for a couple of days. It's urgent. I am helping a Law School friend out."

"What do you mean?"

"Well, it's complicated and dangerous. Let me just say this, we have some powerful people that want something in our possession."

"Our possession?"

"Can you at least tell me what is in *Our Possession*?"

"I guess. We have **Twelve Disc's** that have incriminating information on Alexander Martinorelli. If these discs make it to the FBI it most likely will ruin his financial empire."

"Sonny, why don't you let me help you."

"Absolutely not it is too dangerous. Lisa, you are helping me by taking these assignments. I should only be gone for a few days. I am thinking about leaving tomorrow night."

"Are you sure?"

"I am."

"Well, call me if you change your mind. I'll pick up the assignments tomorrow."

"Thanks."

Later Sonny arrived at the Crown Plaza just in time for dinner. Stephanie had room service delivered and the two of them enjoyed their meal which consisted of shrimp scampi and lobster tails. Stephanie looked into Sonny's eyes and smiled.

"I don't know how I can thank you, Sonny."

"Well, I have a temporary plan until we can get these discs to the FBI."

Sonny got up and walked over to the window looking outside. He was obviously nervous about trying to run from a figure like Alexander Martinorelli, but he was excited he was in Stephanie's life, however long that would be. He turned to Stephanie:

"I will be your bodyguard. We will never be separated. I have a friend, Lisa Taylor, helping me with my business until we get the discs to the FBI. Hopefully, this will only take seventy-two hours or so. We will have to keep moving, changing our appearance, vehicles, until this is completed. I will leave word that I am on a short vacation whereabouts unknown. I think a New York Run will work. New York is laid out and there are a lot of little towns from here to Buffalo. There is a Federal Building there, also. I don't trust anyone in the city. This guy, Martinorelli, is everywhere."

"How long until he can be arrested by the authorities?"

"I don't know for sure. I am waiting for more background information on Martinorelli from the

District Attorney's office. You remember our pal Louie Charles?"

"Good ole Lou. Wait Sonny, what if the District Attorney's office is on Martinorelli's payroll?"

"Then we contact the FBI indirectly through an anonymous tip until we know it is safe to hand over the discs. It is paramount that we get the original discs to the FBI. A copy will not be sufficient."

After dinner the two sat and planned what the next few days would be like. Sonny was adamant that Stephanie never leave his side. She nodded as he made her promise him. He repeatedly told he that one mistake could jeopardize both of their lives. She continued to listen to him.

"Were you to leave my sight for one minute, it would be all that they would need to get you. Stephanie, based on what I already know about Martinorelli, he will do whatever he has to do to stop those discs from going to the authorities. While a lot of his businesses and law firms appear legitimate, there is enough information on those discs to raise significant questions on the legality of some of his operations."

Sonny stood up and reached for his Smart Phone After deleting emails and texts, he looked up at Stephanie.

"At a minimum, a complete investigation into the plethora of businesses should be looked at by the proper authority. Well, I should go. Be packed and I will be here tomorrow night. I would rather travel as much at night as possible. Tomorrow, I will meet with Lou and see what he has on Martinorelli. Please, in the meantime do not answer the door for room service, for anyone. Have your breakfast put outside of your room. Call or text me if you sense that you are in the slightest bit of danger. We will be on our way tomorrow evening. Rest up. The next couple of days will be quite stressful.

Sonny hugged Stephanie tightly. He wanted to stay and spend the night with her, but he had to get his plan rolling. Martinorelli will become more and more desperate each minute they have the discs. He had to get her out of the city ASAP.

"I will be here tomorrow. Be ready."

"I will be."

Stephanie looked at Sonny and they both felt it. Whatever lay ahead for them, they would do it *together.* Whatever Alexander Martinorelli planned on doing to get his discs back would have to go through both of them.

Nine

It was early morning and Alexander Martinorelli had been up for several hours already. After his wife of twenty five years succumbed to cancer he did not like to sleep. He woke up earlier than normal, but could not get back to sleep.

In his mind, he went over again, and again, how Stephanie was able to take his property from his son. How could Michael be so irresponsible to permit this to happen? Because of the negligence of his son, his own life and future rested with the discs.

Shortly after Michael and Stephanie were married, Alexander sensed that something was missing in their marriage. Stephanie, a licensed attorney, worked for a large corporation which had been set up by Alexander. He owned a significant percentage of this corporation. She was paid well and she was somewhat content until she found out that her position in the company was set up by her father-in-law. This was when she first began to question the scope of Alexander's businesses aside from his own National Law Firm.

Stephanie's relationship with Michael began to deteriorate before their wedding. His possessiveness caused her to remain at her Law School one Christmas break during her second year. After a year of marriage, Stephanie believed Michael was not in business meetings, but was with other women. Their sex life just about ended at this time. She felt as if she were more of a possession than a wife.

One evening after Michael was at an alleged business meeting, she had had enough. She went into his study to get on his computer when she noticed that the desk top drawer was slightly ajar. Michael always locked that particular drawer she thought. Stephanie opened the drawer and immediately noticed **Twelve Discs**. After putting one after another into the disc drive, her mouth dropped open.

On these **Twelve Discs**, there were in depth records of every individual on Alexander Martinorelli's payroll. Every corporation, including the one that Stephanie worked at, every politician was clearly evident on these discs. Based on what she observed, there was considerable mention of a *Commission* that he had apparently been a part of for some time now. Her Father-in-law was one of the wealthiest, powerful, influential men in the entire United States, if not the World.

His business interests were substantial and touched most of society in a myriad of ways. His criminal interests were disguised by Dummy Corporations that utilized Wall Street and securities fraud as a major source of income. His illegitimate interests exceeded a power that she could not comprehend. He had a place on the *Commission* which was involved in the business and criminal organizations as Alexander was. Stephanie did not understand anything concerning this *Commission*. She did recall Alexander telling her that the law touches every aspect of life, why not own most of it. This was right before she was going to graduate from Law School.

Stephanie put her hand to her mouth and began to cry after she reviewed all **Twelve Discs**. If Alexander was instrumental to this vast economic and criminal empire, her husband must be a part of it. With all of this power, murder and any other felonious crimes must be components of this empire. She cried because she did not know what to do. The catalog of names included, judges, senators, congressman, mayors, governors, police chiefs, insurance executives, wall street securities officials, bank presidents and union presidents across the United States.

"What are you doing?"

Stephanie turned and looked at Michael who was standing in the doorway. He did not look very happy, He folded his arms.

"Nothing, just checking out a new app."

He looked at her unconvinced. He walked slowly to her side.

"You were told never to use my study. There is critical information that...well it is not for the general public."

Stephanie could not panic. She knew what was on those discs, and Michael was an instrumental part of it all. As afraid as she was she had to become an actress and fast.

"Well, you can come and go as you please and still talk to me like I am a child. Who the hell do you think you are? How many late night meetings this month Michael. I am sick of it. "

Stephanie began to cry softly, but was able to push the eleven remaining discs under the desk out of Michael's line of vision.

"I'm sorry, it's just that I have a lot of important." Michael stopped short.

"What do you mean important?"

"Never mind. Just leave it alone, I'm going to bed."

Stephanie got ready for bed. Michael was soon asleep. She smelled the alcohol on his breath and another woman's perfume. She went to the study and put the twelfth disc with the others in an envelope, and slid them in her briefcase. She knew leaving with the discs was her only recourse now. Michael would figure out soon enough that she knew what was on those discs.

I cannot be part of this family anymore, Stephanie thought. She knew the right thing was to go to, she stopped, where? Alexander Martinorelli was everywhere. She quickly packed some clothes and quietly drove away. *What now?* She thought as she sobbed. It was then that she thought of Sonny Thomas. ***I have to get these Twelve Discs to Sonny, he will know what to do.***

Ten

Sonny arrived at the restaurant around lunch time. He politely asked the waitress for a cup of coffee as he awaited his lunch companion. Louie Charles arrived shortly thereafter. Louie did not look himself.

"What the hell happened to you?"

"Sonny, you're in serious trouble if you help Stephanie out."

"Why is that?"

"Including the **Twelve Discs** that we watched together, I went beyond the District Attorney's office. This guy is everywhere. He is influential and more powerful than he is wealthy. He is a member of the *Commission*. Do you know who they represent?"

"A little, most of it hearsay. A ruling board that controls part of the criminal and economic empires that exist today. Like I said, I don't know too much detail."

"Sonny, the *Commission* does not only represent the criminal element of the United States, it has advanced and controls wall street, banking, securities, anything that has economic ramifications for the balance of our population. Interest rates, global conflicts are within their control. These individual members have power never witnessed before. They not only control what the former underworld controlled, they have evolved and now their members include world bankers and other ultra-powerful families. They decide who will win elections, what the interest rate will be worldwide, who we go to war with. Stay away, Sonny, you cannot win."

"I can't Lou. I gave my word to Stephanie."

"This Martinorelli guy has a clean record. Zero arrests in his lifetime. There is not even a hint that he has ever received a parking ticket. Now do you want to hear the bad news?"

"Can't wait."

"He controls the police in strategic positions in the State of New York. Sheriff Departments, State Police, they all have some connection to him. There is some probability that he has even infiltrated the FBI."

Sonny drank his coffee trying to hide the fear that he now had. He ordered a second cup of coffee. He listened to his buddy.

"He is supposedly self-made and began his ascent at an early age. Coincidentally, his boss, Pete Fabruguzzio, became missing at that time. Never to be found. Anything you fear, this guy controls. It never ends.

Sonny, how can you not only avoid, but run from such an individual?"

"I never said it would be easy. The FBI may have some compromised agents on his payroll, but not the entire agency. Were the FBI to have custody of these **Twelve** original **Discs**, I believe justice will prevail. I just have to make certain that it gets to the right special agent."

"Sonny, he will ruin you."

"Not if I get him first."

Alexander and Michael looked at police chief Roger Fordrani, awaiting a response.

"Well, I have nothing to report as of yet. I have people at his residence and office."

"Not good enough Roger," replied Michael.

"Look, I sent two of Rocco's men to meet and discuss the situation with Mr. Sonny Thomas. He has been warned not to get involved, or else. The sister of your daughter-in law met with Thomas yesterday. Something is up because we cannot find out where the sister is."

"Gentlemen, we must get Stephanie before she leaves New York. If this Sonny Thomas character is helping Stephanie pay a visit to his office. Every second that passes we reduce our chances of getting those discs back."

Alexander Martinorelli circled Fordrani stopping directly in front of him. He just glared at the Police Commissioner making Fordrani very nervous.

"Roger once she gets out of New York the more difficult it will be to get my discs back."

"I'm on it 24/7. I promise I will not let you down. You have my word."

"Actually Roger, your life depends on it. Get going. I am sending Tony Elia with you. Go to every possible location she may be. Needless to say time is of the essence."

Roger Fordrani would never return as he was now part of the plan to expedite getting the discs back from Stephanie. His failure to get her was unacceptable.

———————

Later, Sonny arrived at the hotel as it was getting dark. Wearing a disguise, a hotel maintenance uniform, he knocked on Stephanie's hotel room door.

"Who is it?"

"Hurry up it's me."

Once inside, after a quick hug and kiss, Sonny handed Stephanie a short black wig and a hotel maid's uniform. They left. When they arrived in the lobby of the Crown Plaza, they spoke louder than usual and acted like two employees leaving work. A cab had been waiting.

"JFK Airport, as fast as you can."

Upon arrival at JFK the two found the car and sped Westbound towards Central New York. The two of them kept their disguises on. While it would take longer traveling by automobile it would be safer. Plus, he knew exactly where Stephanie was at all times.

"Sonny, how long until we get these disc's to the FBI?"

"Not sure yet."

"We have to get them to the FBI, right?"

"Yes, but we have to insulate ourselves from Alexander and Michael. They must be desperate as it has been a few days and they were unable to find you. We have to copy the disc's and get the original discs to the proper FBI Special Agent. Unfortunately, the old man may have a spy in the FBI."

"This guy is something else I tell you. His connections are everywhere."

"It definitely makes what we're doing more difficult, how could it not, but there has to be some special agent that is honest and not on his payroll. We will keep trying until we find the right special agent. If half of what I observed on those disc's is accurate, the Martinorelli family will be history. His place on the *Commission* will be in jeopardy as well."

"Sonny, I am scared to death right now. I did not mean for you to become involved in such an impossible situation."

"Too late for that. Alexander must be panicking. When you panic you make mistakes. He will come after us with everything he has. I doubt he will be reactive in this situation. He has too many weapons and too much power."

Sonny Thomas drove at a good clip on Route 81 Westbound traveling towards Binghamton, New York, not knowing who was chasing him. It was autumn and the leaves had already begun to change their foliage.

Stephanie Martinorelli was sound asleep leaning her head on Sonny's shoulder. He thought to himself what a difference a few days can make. The present situation had the two of them on the run from one of the most powerful figures in the United States; who happened to be her father-in-law.

Alexander Martinorelli was a member of the **Commission**, one of the elite political, business and criminal memberships in the United States. This group contained only thirty-six members who were placed strategically in various parts of the United States and controlled everything.

Due to some negligence, and, or, carelessness on the part of Michael Martinorelli, the husband of Stephanie, and son of Alexander, Stephanie was able to take possession of **Twelve Discs'** that contained every facet of the Martinorelli Empire including their payroll. These discs' had judges, politicians, senators, police officials, and prominent business people throughout the United States on the Martinorelli payroll. After perusing the discs' Stephanie knew that if her husband or father-in-law knew that she gained access to or had any knowledge of the contents of the discs' her life would be in jeopardy. Now on the run with the assistance of Sonny Thomas, they planned to make a New York Run from the Martinorelli Empire, until they could get the discs' to the proper authority. At this point the primary focus was on survival until this could be accomplished.

Stephanie stirred a little then woke up smiling at the exhausted Sonny. She smiled at him. Sonny looked at her and how beautiful she was.

"Well good evening, I mean morning Steph."

It was in the middle of the night and Sonny had been driving for hours. The traffic on Route 81 was relatively light and Sonny was making great time.

"I'm hungry. Can we stop and eat?"

"Sure. I could use a coffee. I'll stop at the next restaurant on the highway. You OK?"

"I still cannot believe all of this is happening. It is very surreal. I am scared, but also happy you are with me."

"I know exactly what you mean."

Sonny stared at Stephanie, she was even beautiful as she just woke up. Black wig and all. There was no question about his feelings for her. The question was how she felt for him.

"There's a diner."

"Yeah, I see it."

Neither were aware of the Lincoln Town Car that was ten miles behind them driven by Tony Elia and his passenger, Police Chief Roger Fordrani.

Eleven

Earlier at the New York City FBI Headquarters, Special Agent C.J. Jeffers was filling out his latest paperwork. Jeffers, age forty-two, African-American was 6 foot 2 and weighed two hundred twenty-five pounds. He was athletic and still lifted weights on a regular basis. He still played basketball one day a week.

C.J. graduated from Law School and after one uneventful year of general practice decided to go after his lifelong dream of being a special agent for the FBI. He went to Quantico for his training and had been a successful agent for the past fifteen years.

His biggest disappointment was two failed attempts to arrest Alexander Martinorelli. On both surveillance efforts the results failed to incriminate Martinorelli on any possible criminal activity. Jeffers was still convinced that there was something not right with Martinorelli. He just could not prove it.

C.J. Jeffers had evidence that Martinorelli was one of the select members of the *Commission*. A group that controlled not only the criminal element nationwide, but economic control of Wall Street through securities fraud and a plethora of illicit businesses. This *Commission* was a very powerful, impenetrable organization that utilized all of their power and all their weapons.

Special Agent C.J. Jeffers finally concluded that Martinorelli must have connections with local police departments, sheriff departments, state police, and, even the FBI to be able to evade any prosecution to date. He would never give up as he believed his assertion of Alexander Martinorelli was correct.

"Sir," shouted Special Agent Evan Huntington.

"I thought you would like to know that it has come to my attention that the daughter-in-law of Alexander Martinorelli has been officially reported missing."

Special Agent Jeffers stood up and stared into the wall. He rubbed his goatee. Has the old man finally made a mistake, he hoped.

"Huntington, let's get someone on this. Someone who is very good at missing persons."

He thought that if Alexander Martinorelli had finally made a mistake he would be ready to take advantage of the situation. It seemed too good to be true. He smiled. He would not get his hopes up yet. He needed more facts and quick.

"Put someone very trustworthy on this, Evan. I cannot make a mistake with this guy. Hopefully the third time will be a charm."

While Sonny and Stephanie were being seated at the restaurant the Lincoln Town Car sped past the diner. Tony Elia drove and Police Chief, Roger Fordrani sat in the passenger seat. Both men were tired and hungry.

"I'm getting a little hungry. How about you?" asked Fordrani.

"I'm always hungry," replied Tony Elia.

"Next restaurant, we'll stop."

"OK Chief."

"The Boss wants us to check every possible place she may be. He also thinks that Sonny Thomas may be involved somehow. The background on Thomas indicates that he is originally from Western New York."

"Well, we will check every possible rest stop along the way. Besides, almost every state police vehicle on Route 90 will be on the lookout for them."

"Chief, there is a truck stop. Let's eat."

"Good idea."

Special Agent C.J. Jeffers perused the paperwork in front of him. Stephanie Martinorelli, a lawyer, married to Michael Martinorelli, son of Alexander Martinorelli – MISSING.

Also missing, or presumed missing, is Sonny Thomas, a former Law School colleague of Stephanie Martinorelli. Why? Both had clean records, both licensed attorneys. Thomas was a licensed private investigator. There had to be something between these two he thought.

"Evan, let's put surveillance on Alexander Martinorelli's office and residences. We have to speak with any friend or relative that knows Sonny Thomas and Stephanie Martinorelli."

C.J. Jeffers thought to himself. She must have something incriminating against the old man. Why else would she be missing? Was she on the run? Was she dead? He did not know how Sonny Thomas was involved at this point. He would investigate this matter more fully.

Sonny sat at the diner looking intently at Stephanie. He was concerned about the danger the two were in, but he was with her.

"Steph, the information on the disc's will definitely incriminate Alexander Martinorelli and any member of his organization. Based on what I observed, the entire payroll of his organization is on these **Twelve Discs.** Why? Why would anyone in his position reduce all of his businesses, illicit or licit to twelve discs?"

"Sonny, remember, it wasn't just anyone. It was his sole heir, Michael. He was inattentive and was not really concerned that anyone, especially me, could have ever gotten access to the discs."

"I guess he underestimated you. Big time."

The waitress walked over and gave Sonny pancakes and sausage. She gave Stephanie a cheese omelet and refilled both of their coffees. It was still dark. They talked as they wolfed down their meals.

"I have to be able to copy or burn the discs. Once I am comfortable with a special agent at the FBI, I will somehow get the original discs to someone I one-hundred percent trust at the FBI. Once the original discs are secure we will try and avoid Martinorelli and his goons until the authorities get them. Once the FBI has the original discs they can arrest Martinorelli. Our job will be complete."

"It sounds great to me in theory, it is just that there is danger everywhere. His organization is lethal. I just want this over, Sonny. As long as Alexander knows we have the discs, our lives' are in jeopardy."

"Don't worry Steph. We will be in contact with the FBI before you know it. Then this will be over."

Stephanie did not want her and Sonny to be over. He had been out of her life too long already. They got up, Sonny left a fifty dollar bill and left the restaurant. Sonny drove towards Binghamton, New York, Westbound on Route 81.

Twelve

Alexander Martinorelli's organization had been impenetrable. **Until Now**. Since he took over for Pete Fabruguzzio in 1975, forty plus years ago, he slyly and cunningly acquired business after business. With all of the vigor, ambition and intelligence of a chief executive officer, he achieved a business and criminal conglomerate unmatched.

His Law Firm became National. He was as untouchable as anyone with that vast amount of power and wealth. Finally, as a member of the *Commission*, he appeared to be in total control of his organization and life.

Now that Stephanie had complete access to his payroll throughout the United States, his organization was, for the first time, susceptible to being exposed to the proper authorities. While Alexander had achieved extraordinary success in his licit businesses, he achieved a similar success in his illicit businesses. That was the problem.

Alexander thought to himself that he must utilize all of his power to prevent those discs from being turned over to the FBI, or he would be finished. The *Commission*, the actual only board he answers to, would never let him bring any unnecessary publicity that may damage their reputation or jeopardize their future in any way. With the Fordrani plan soon to be accomplished he needed a more complete strategy to catch his daughter-in law before it was too late.

"Mr. Martinorelli," called Jordyn his blonde, blue-eyed secretary.

"Yes, Jordyn what is it?"

"Mr. Rocco is here with some associates."

"Send them in."

Rocco and three of Alexander's associate's walked in the office. The four men greeted their boss and then sat down.

"Rocco, my trusted and loyal friend, thank you for coming so soon."

"Boss, here are three of the best men I have. They are superior button men and they have the utmost respect for you. Their loyalty to you is unmatched. All three are eager to do whatever is necessary to assist you in this unfortunate situation."

One by one Rocco introduced the three men and handed paperwork to Alexander going over every pertinent trait of each of their backgrounds.

Salvatore Puzero:

Born in Little Italy, New York, thirty years old and had been on the Martinorelli payroll since he was twenty-one years old. Initially, he assisted in lower level criminal activity including loan sharking, collections for unions and most recently becoming involved in securities fraud for Martinorelli. He was a button man on five separate occasions and was successful on each one of them. He was an up and comer. He wanted more responsibility and more money under the direction of his Capo, Rocco. Salvatore was a sociopath and was very proficient on any job he was ordered to fulfill. His temper was legendary.

Jimmy Degregorio (A.K.A. Jimmy Death) :

Born in Buffalo, New York, started late into his thirties when he came to work for the Martinorelli organization. He previously worked for a former under boss in Buffalo, New York, who was now known worldwide for his pizza and chicken wings.

Jimmy ran the rackets and was very good at making a profit no matter what type of job. He was an organizational gold mine. He worked all of the restaurants in the area and became a top earner. Jimmy had three hits on his resume, one a local restaurant owner who refused to pay the twenty percent increase on his collection. This restaurant owner had to be made an example of. Jimmy only carried a knife. Never a gun. He was very ambitious always looking for an opportunity to grow within the family.

Petey Mancini:

Born in Little Italy, New York was with the Martinorelli organization since he was sixteen years old. He also was a sociopath and did whatever he had to, to remain loyal to the Martinorelli organization. He had previously been responsible for car bombings, structural damage to buildings and murder with his bare hands. His temper along with his physical strength was almost impossible to conquer. At 6 foot 5 and over 300 pounds he was a wrecking ball. He had been pinched three times. Overall, he did two stints in prison and just recently got out. Petey was all about the Martinorelli organization and was eager to assist Alexander Martinorelli about anything. He often teared up in the presence of Alexander because of his enormous loyalty and love for his boss.

After briefing the three gentlemen on what he wanted achieved Alexander walked around his office. He eventually grabbed a cup of espresso and sat down. He looked at the three men intently.

"Gentleman, I need these discs' back as soon as possible. Stephanie took my property from Michael and I believe Sonny Thomas is assisting her in getting these discs' to the FBI. This cannot happen. It will ruin my organization. Rocco will give you three the specific plan that I personally devised. Each of you will travel to three separate parts of New York and you should be able to get my discs from them. I have one hundred percent faith that you will be successful."

The three men nodded not saying a word and stood up simultaneously. Petey Mancini's eyes filled with tears.

"For doing this service for me, you will be wealthier than you can ever have imagined. When you check your checking accounts, it is not a mistake. That is yours with a lot more to come. After this is all over, I have positions for all three of you in my licit, corporate world."

The three men just looked at Alexander with reverence, and, again, just nodded, their loyalty apparent to Alexander and his organization.

"Whatever you have to do to get those discs back to me is of no vital concern to me. If the two of them have to disappear, make it as clean as possible. Now go to Jordyn, she will give you keys, credit cards and cash advances."

After the door closed, Alexander sat with Rocco and discussed the importance of getting the disc's before they could be turned over to the FBI. Rocco listened to every word his boss spoke with his hands on his knees.

"If I am out of business so are some very influential people who will turn their heads, rather than incriminate themselves. Contact our backups with the local and state police authorities. Make sure Fordrani has done his job."

"Will do so, Boss."

"Oh yeah, one other thing, check our sources with the local FBI and see if they know anything that may help."

"Mr. Martinorelli, don't worry. With all of your connections, she doesn't stand a chance."

"I wish that I was as confident as you."

Sonny continued Westbound on Route 81 heading towards Binghamton, New York. After catching a couple hours of sleep at a rest stop after their middle of the night breakfast, they both felt better. It was getting light.

"Steph."

"Yes?"

"Other than Michael and your Father-in-law, how many associates of the Martinorelli organization would you be able to recognize?"

"I'm not sure, but at least a couple of dozen if not by name than by faces."

"The reason I ask is that along with the police, sheriff's department and state police, he'll probably send some bulls after us like the two that visited me yesterday."

Stephanie did not say a word. Sonny looked at her. He grabbed the back of her neck and rubbed it. Stephanie just lightly moaned her approval.

"Binghamton, thirty miles, we'll grab a hotel, shower and then change cars later."

"Sounds good to me."

Evan Huntington placed the name of Sarah Dempsey in front of C.J. Jeffers. He looked at Huntington.

"This is the only living relative of Stephanie Martinorelli, her identical twin sister, Sarah Dempsey. I contacted Sonny Thomas' secretary and she hesitated at first, but gave me the out of town hotel she was staying at. She wouldn't budge until I informed her that the FBI was on their side."

"Let's pay Ms. Dempsey a visit. We have to figure out what is going on here."

After the special agent gently knocked, the hotel door opened.

"Good morning, Ms. Dempsey, this is Special Agent, Evan Huntington, and I am Special Agent C.J. Jeffers from the New York City's FBI Office. We were wondering if we could speak to you regarding your twin sister, Stephanie Martinorelli."

Sarah Dempsey, obviously uncomfortable, invited them in and offered them a cup of coffee. She glanced at both men crossing her arms.

"Why is the FBI interested in my sister?"

"To be quite candid Ms. Dempsey, we believe that your sister is on the run from the Alexander Martinorelli organization. We believe a Private Investigator, Sonny Thomas, is assisting your sister as she is most likely in great danger. We don't know why she is missing. That is why we came to speak with you."

"Yesterday, no, two days ago, I went and spoke with Sonny Thomas at his office early in the morning. I gave him all of the information that I had regarding Stephanie. I told him, I never trusted Michael Martinorelli, or his family for that matter."

"Did you speak to Stephanie before her disappearance?" asked special agent Evan Huntington.

"The last time I spoke with my sister, she was upset about something. She would not elaborate on what, specifically, was bothering her. On many occasions she mentioned Sonny Thomas and Law School. She had told me that they had a brief romance at the end of their Law School days. After Stephanie was missing for two days, I recalled Stephanie mentioning to me that if she were ever missing to contact Sonny Thomas. So I did. I went to his office without an appointment and gave him all I knew about Stephanie. Sonny Thomas said he had an idea where she may be. He arranged for me to get out of town until this is all over."

Sarah paused and wiped a tear from her eye. Special Agent, Evan Huntington handed her a Kleenex. She sat up and walked around the room.

"I understand how upset this can be for you, Ms. Dempsey."

"You really do not. That Martinorelli family or business, whatever you want to call them are too rich and powerful to let Stephanie have something on them. I don't trust her father-in-law, the husband I just don't like. Is Stephanie ever going to be found alive?"

Sarah continued to cry softly looking at a picture of Stephanie and herself from high school that she brought with her to the hotel.

"Anything else, Ms. Dempsey? Why, again, did you contact Sonny Thomas? There are hundreds of private investigation firms in New York."

"Like I said, I spoke with Stephanie and she was edgy and nervous. I asked her what was wrong and she told me, 'Sarah, if I ever turn up missing contact Sonny Thomas. He will be the only person in the world that would be able to find me.' "

"Interesting," said Jeffers.

"Anything else?" asked Even Huntington.

"No, as soon as I thought Stephanie was missing, I went to see Sonny Thomas. As twins we spoke to each other every day of our lives. I knew after the second day that something was wrong. That is when I went to see Sonny Thomas and told him that my sister was missing."

"Again, that was two days ago?"

"OK, well thank you Ms. Dempsey for that information."

Sarah looked helpless and teared up again. She walked to the window trying to hide her tears.

"We will do anything we can to locate your twin sister. Stephanie and Sonny are our top priority."

Special Agent C.J. Jeffers walked around the room. He said nothing. Finally, he said,

"When Stephanie gets in touch with you, or if she gets in touch with you, call me directly. Here is my personal cell phone."

"She will be alright, I promise," said Special Agent Huntington.

Once in the car, C.J. Jeffers told Evan to get two bodyguards on Sarah Dempsey immediately. The Special Agent complied with his request from his supervisor. C.J.

Jeffers tried to figure out what Stephanie had on the Martinorelli organization, but he drew a blank.

"Let's get an FBI background on Sonny Thomas. This guy seems too good to be true. Why put yourself in this amount of danger and drama over a former Law School friend?"

Thirteen

Sonny laid both suitcases on the floor of the hotel room. Stephanie eyed the two double beds. They each only had one suitcase and started to unpack their belongings.

"I think I'll grab a quick shower and then try to sleep for a few hours. The next couple of days will be rough."

"OK Sonny, I can shower after you."

Sonny put his face directly at the shower head and let the water blast away at his face. He was thinking how he could pull this off and keep the two of them alive. One step at a time is the only way he thought. With barely a sound, Stephanie slipped into the shower with Sonny. She embraced Sonny from behind. Sonny turned around and gazed into Stephanie's eyes.

"I worry more about you than I do myself, Steph."

"Sonny, I don't know where I would be right now without your help."

The two embraced both looking at various parts of the shower. Sonny grabbed her chin and kissed her lovingly. The proceeded to make love as passionately as they did years earlier during that last week of Law School. Eventually, the two made it to one of the double beds, and fell asleep in each others arms.

A few hours later, Sonny awoke with Stephanie in his arms. He looked at the clock in the hotel room. Sonny shook Stephanie awake.

"Steph, we should get up. It's getting late."

"OK."

"I'll put some coffee on and order room service."

Sonny kissed her on the lips. She grabbed the back of his neck kissing him back.

"Really Steph, we should get going. Trust me, I would rather stay in bed with you, forever. Hopefully, that time will come soon."

"Are you making a commitment Mr. Thomas?"

"I have been in love with you since the first time we met, our first year of Law School. Even though you were engaged, I always felt that we were right for each other. Then the last couple days of Law School confirmed to me that we should be together. Those days were the highlight of my life. I really thought you would leave Michael for me after those couple of wonderful days. When I read that note, I was heartbroken."

"I am very sorry for that. It was so perfect being with you those couple of days. I was torn, and I really considered calling Michael and breaking off the engagement. I really did. I just thought, were I to leave Michael, he would make it his mission to make the rest of my life miserable."

"He sort of did that anyway, hasn't he?"

"Not if we can get these discs to the proper authorities."

There was a knock on the hotel door. Sonny put his finger to his lips. He walked over and looked into the peephole.

"Yes?"

"Room service."

"Please just leave it outside of my door. I am grabbing some clothes."

"Sure thing."

The hotel waiter left their meals outside the hotel door. Sonny opened the door and checked down both hallways. He pulled the wheeled cart into the center of their room. They began to eat their meal.

"Steph, I have already made an arrangements to switch to several other vehicles. We'll continue to travel while it is dark out. The more inconspicuous we are, the better."

"Sonny, it was not easy for me to leave that note. I was very confused because I was engaged, but there you were. I tried to fight it, but when I saw how emotional you were my heart told me to spend time with you before it was too late. After I left the note, I cried for a week because I missed you. I just did not think that we would end up as a couple."

"Somehow, some way I will figure a way out of this mess, and then we can talk about us."

The two ate their meals quickly and then showered. Separate this time. They dressed, packed, and were ready to go. Once in the new vehicle Sonny looked at Stephanie.

"I am thinking about trying a test tomorrow on the FBI. See if we can by chance find someone not on the Martinorelli payroll. We may have to try a couple of times."

"Where are we headed now?"

"Elmira. We have to zig and zag as much as possible to avoid whoever is after us. We have to move steadily, but go through these small towns. We cannot afford to make one mistake. We will copy the discs as I already explained. At the right time we will give the original **Twelve Discs** to the proper FBI Special Agent. When or how, I still do not know."

"You ready Steph?"

"I am."

"Let's go."

Fourteen

Earlier, Tony Elia and Roger Fordrani arrived in Binghamton, New York. They checked into a local franchise hotel. They relaxed an hour or so and then went to lunch.

"I have never observed Alexander like this, Tony. I am actually a little nervous about the entire matter."

"Well, he has a lot at stake. She took something that did not belong to her. I would be worried if I was in his place also."

Tony Elia thought to himself how easy it would be to end Fordrani's life and blame it on Stephanie and that Private Investigator character, Sonny Thomas. He had never in all his years on the Martinorelli payroll observed a police official that was this incompetent and utterly useless. His demise was well earned.

"They both have to come out into plain sight sometime. Then all of the coppers I have looking for them will inevitably get them and finally get the old man's property back where it belongs."

"Chief, Rocco gave specific instructions that we contact the local powers to be when we arrive here. We need as many people looking for them as possible."

" Let's do it, Tony."

Salvatore Puzero drove twenty miles past the speed limit as he headed Westbound on the I-90. His destination was Western New York. There was a Federal Building in Buffalo and the old man thought that area should be covered. Once he arrived there, he would meet with some local associates of the Boss.

Salvatore had heard of his Buffalo associate, but he had never met him personally. This particular associate had run things for the Martinorelli organization for over twenty years. The associate was very loyal to Martinorelli. Salvatore had been waiting for an opportunity like this for years. He would not disappoint Mr. Martinorelli.

Jimmy Degregorio (Jimmy D) also drove at a good clip on the I-90. His destination was an hour or so east of Buffalo – Rochester, New York. There was a Federal building there and Martinorelli wanted that area covered also. He was to meet with some associates of the Martinorelli organization that handled Rochester, Syracuse, and Central New York. Jimmy D wanted to be the one that took care of this matter personally, with his infamous knife.

Petey Mancini sat in his apartment waiting for a call from Michael Martinorelli. Petey's background included car bombings and anything that had to do with explosives. He was a loose cannon.

The Martinorelli organization had recently learned that a close friend of both Stephanie and Sonny's worked at the District Attorney's Office in the Bronx. He was being watched very closely by someone on the Martinorelli payroll. Petey worked with Michael Martinorelli before as he was always on call for his boss.

Around the same time, Michael had a meeting with his Father, who had called him to meet at his office. Rocco as usual was present.

"Soon, Michael, we start closing in on those two. Tony will handle a matter in Binghamton that will turn the tide in our favor. Hopefully, the discs will be back in my possession within the next twenty-four hours."

"What's the plan, Pop?"

"I can't tell you everything Michael, but by tomorrow we won't be the only organization chasing Stephanie and Sonny Thomas. They will be considered criminals with an APB (All

Points Bulletin) being issued throughout New York State."

Earlier, Roger Fordrani and Tony Elia were all over Binghamton, but there was no luck or sighting of either Stephanie or Sonny. They checked every possible hotel or motel in the area.

After hours of searching for the two, they decided to go to dinner as it was getting dark. Then they would report to the Boss what they did not do and retire for the evening.

The dinner was at a local Italian restaurant and they both drank red wine throughout the meal. As they left the restaurant, they walked to the Lincoln Town Car. Police Chief, Roger Fordrani, never saw it coming. As the two men casually walked to their vehicle, Tony maintained a step behind the Police Chief. Tony then stopped, and with his 45 put two shots into the back of Fordrani head, killing him instantly. He dropped to the ground like a sack of potatoes.

Within minutes, the local Binghamton Police Department arrived to the scene. After hours of statement taking and witness canvassing, it was reported to the local news and went viral on the internet that two individuals were identified to be prime suspects in the murder of New York City Police Chief, Roger Fordrani. Two pictures were shown, one being Stephanie Martinorelli and the other, Sonny Thomas.

Fifteen

Sonny and Stephanie arrived in Elmira a few hours later. Sonny took every side road he could, intentionally avoiding main thoroughfares. It was dark, and they planned on changing cars again in Elmira. Their final destination was Buffalo, New York. There was a Federal Building located downtown. After they changed cars, they stopped at an all-night rest stop. Sonny filled the new vehicle with gas.

Stephanie looked at her Smart Phone and did not believe what she read. The text from the local news stated:

> *The murder of New York City, Police Chief Roger Fordrani has the city of Binghamton in an uproar. Two shots to the back of the head assassination style are presumed to be the cause of death. Local police have an APB on two New York City attorneys', Stephanie Martinorelli, and Sonny Thomas. There is a statewide search for the two suspects who are considered armed and dangerous. Chief Fordrani was in Binghamton visiting relatives. He was a fine police officer and will be missed.*

Stephanie showed the article to Sonny. He had to read it a second time. He dropped his arms to his side.

"Unbelievable. This guy will stop at nothing to get those discs back. He'll even commit murder to get us. We have to move. *Now*."

The two went back to the car and drove away. Speeding was not an option because of all the police agencies on Martinorelli's payroll. Sonny thought, it was bad enough having the entire Martinorelli organization chasing after them. Now the balance of the population might recognize them, even though they were in disguise still, and, assist Martinorelli, indirectly, in getting to them. An APB was no joke. Every law abiding citizen might recognize them as murderers of a Police Chief since their faces were all over the internet, television, and soon to be newspapers nationwide. He just raised the ante, Sonny thought.

Special Agent C.J. Jeffers looked at Evan Huntington. The text they received from FBI Headquarters in Washington D.C. indicated that Police Chief, Roger Fordrani, was murdered assassination style. The prime suspects are Sonny

Thomas and Stephanie Martinorelli. C.J. Jeffers sighed loudly. He filled up his cup of coffee.

"There is something about this that does not add up. If they are on the run, why would they bring more attention to themselves by committing a Capital murder? A New York City Police Chief? I don't see any logical motive."

C.J. Jeffers stood up and walked out toward his window. He gazed outside and just shook his head. He turned around suddenly and addressed his colleague.

"They must have some incriminating information on Martinorelli. The old man can't find them and now he is panicking hoping this murder will bring them to him quicker."

"I agree," said Huntington.

"This is just too convenient for the Martinorelli organization. They can't get to them, so they set them up and have a statewide APB on them instead. The information they have must be able to dismantle his empire. We have to get to them first."

"Huntington, we somehow have to communicate with Stephanie and Sonny, letting them know that the FBI is on their side."

"Sir, why don't we proceed like we also are after them? When we have the opportunity we can then let them know where we really stand."

"I like it Huntington. Let's get out that given the present situation, the FBI believes that it would be to their advantage to surrender immediately to the FBI. Throw my name in there, maybe Thomas will read between the lines. Evan, this is between you and me. We have to get Martinorelli now."

"Got it sir."

Sonny left Elmira and was now heading westbound on every country road that he recalled from his youth. It was very monotonous, but safer.

"Early tomorrow I am going to try and get in touch with an honest FBI Special Agent. With all of the connections and influence the old man has, every police agency in New York will be on the lookout for us. I know I have said it before, but we cannot make one mistake. Even more so now than before this Binghamton murder."

"Sonny, we must be getting to him that he would murder someone on his payroll."

"I agree. My cell phone is untraceable, but for how long I'm not sure. I have three on me all the time. When we stop I'll make three copies of the **Twelve Discs.**"

"Why would you make three copies?"

"Remember how important it is to establish the original when there was any issue regarding proper chain of custody. Federal Rules of Evidence. When the time is ripe we cannot let his team of lawyers have this evidence thrown out because we did not establish a proper chain of custody or can prove that we have the original **Twelve Discs**."

"I almost forgot how you absolutely loved evidence in Law School."

"My favorite class in Law School. Hopefully, it will help us now."

Tomorrow will definitely be a big day, thought Sonny Thomas. I'll be able to start leaking information to the FBI. He continued to drive through the night.

Sixteen

"Hello, this is the New York City FBI, how can I assist you today?"

"Yes, I would like to know the procedure for reporting a laundry list of crimes," stated Sonny.

"This is Special Agent Williams, what kind of crimes are you reporting?"

"You name the crime and Alexander Martinorelli is involved, and has been involved, with these myriad of crimes since the 1970's."

The Special Agent's eyes opened wide.

"Can I please have your name sir?"

"I am someone without a name. Contact a supervisor and explain that I personally have enough tangible evidence to put Martinorelli away for good. They won't even ask, they will know who I am."

Sonny hung up the phone in hopes that this information would get to an honest special agent. This was the first step in getting the original **Twelve Discs** to the FBI.

Lisa Taylor never really paid attention to the news on the Radio, normally she listened to music. When she heard the allegations against Sonny and Stephanie she listened closely and turned the volume up.

'Last night in Binghamton, New York, Police Chief, Roger Fordrani was murdered assassination style. Eyewitnesses had described the prime suspects as Sonny Thomas and Stephanie Martinorelli of New York. An APB has been put out state wide on these two suspects.'

Lisa shut off the radio and sped to Sonny's office. I have to help him regardless of what he told me she thought. As Lisa walked into the office, Ashley in tears stated,

"Oh, Lisa, have you heard the news yet? The police and FBI are on their way over. They just called."

"I heard it on the radio. I didn't even check my Smart Phone today. I don't believe a word of it."

Sonny never told Lisa any specifics of how he would get a copy of the discs to the FBI. She knew this was to protect her, but now it angered her because she did not know what to do to help Sonny and Stephanie. She tried to put herself in Sonny's shoes and then she heard a loud knock on the office's front door. Lisa backed into Sonny's office.

"Good morning." Ashley said.

"Can I help you?"

Two large Italian men walked inside the office. They had already visited Sonny.

"Yeah you can help us. Where is Sonny Thomas and Stephanie Martinorelli?"

One of the men, the same one who threw the chair against the wall, violently ripped the phone wire out of the wall. Hearing this, Lisa cleverly backed into a closet and shut the door behind her without a sound. Lisa then heard Ashley scream at the top of her lungs until she then heard nothing. After hearing the door slam shut, she waited a minute or two and then walked into the office area.

Ashley was gone, apparently kidnapped by two associates of Alexander Martinorelli.

Seventeen

Special Agent Williams phoned the New York FBI office, and after several transfers heard,

"This is Special Agent Jeffers, how can I help you?"

"Yes, I received a call earlier, sir. Probably a wacko that said that he had a laundry list of crimes to report that somehow are connected to Alexander Martinorelli."

"Anything else? Like a name?"

"Sir, do you think it has any validity?"

"You never know. No idea who the caller was?"

"No. Oh yeah. He said you would know who he was, and that he would eventually call you."

Jeffers hung up the phone. No doubt about it, this was Sonny Thomas, but why didn't he just say who he was? For some reason it appears Thomas does not trust the FBI, at least not yet. He called Huntington on his office phone.

Unbeknownst to Special Agent Williams or Jeffers, Special Agent Damian Parker hung up the phone after listening to the prior conversation. He took a cigarette break and called the home office of Alexander Martinorelli and Associates. Within minutes this information had been conveyed to the old man.

"Well, I am not surprised, we figured they would try and get the FBI involved. Have our contact get as close to the situation as he can without drawing any attention. It's time he earned his paycheck from us."

After deliberating back and forth how to proceed Jeffers gave his instructions to Huntington. Number one, find out who the mole is in the FBI on Martinorelli's payroll. Number two, check and see if any of his recent calls were third partied in. Finally, he wanted the FBI background check on Sonny Thomas.

C.J. Jeffers perused the background check not saying a word just occasionally shaking his head up and down on an intermittent basis. Evan Huntington walked into the office.

"Clean, honest a genuine good guy with not even a parking ticket. Why would he risk his entire life on a former Law School friend? I don't get it."

"Huntington, who was the other friend Sonny and Stephanie had the study group with?"

"Louis Charles. He is an assistant District Attorney in the Bronx."

"Let's set a meeting up with him ASAP. I need to know a little more about Sonny and Stephanie. Maybe this DA can enlighten us on what is between these two. I almost forgot Huntington, how is the surveillance going on the old man?"

"Nothing yet."

"Let me know if anything suspicious is observed. I think the old man is beyond desperate, given the Binghamton situation and now the kidnapping. Now would be a perfect time to finally put him away."

Eighteen

Michael Martinorelli was confused. He knew that he was really not in love with Stephanie, his infidelity spoke volumes about that. She was, however, his wife. Who is this Sonny Thomas character and why would he jeopardize everything for Stephanie. The offer his father gave him would have set him up for a lifetime. He immediately thought about the one Christmas she stayed at school. She mentioned the name every so often, but Michael never thought anything of it.

Until now.

He had a meeting with Petey Mancini to discuss a situation that had to be addressed almost immediately. Louis Charles, a Bronx assistant District Attorney, was a friend of both Sonny and Stephanie. He would assist them given the opportunity. That would not be possible according to his plan for the DA.

Michael knew that he let his father down and would never be forgiven or thought of in the same esteem of the old man. He was not as smart as his father and never completed college. Stephanie was his trophy to prove to the world that he had what it takes to be successful. Now with the present situation he felt alone and utterly useless. He had to do something to win his father back. He focused on Stephanie and her betrayal by taking something that was not hers. While he was negligent in not locking his desk as was his usual custom, she still took something that was not hers. His cell phone rang.

"Yeah. OK meet me at the Bronx District Attorney's office. I have a job for you."

"Michael, I will be there within the hour."

Lisa Taylor could not sit still and not do anything. Ashley was kidnapped by some of Alexander Martinorelli associates right in front of her. Normally she would call Sonny and they would figure a plan. She just froze. Enough of this, she thought to herself.

She found herself driving at an alarming rate of speed and could not stop her hands from shaking. She did not know what to do and where to turn now that Sonny was gone. She could not contact the police for obvious reasons. She could not contact Sonny, who knew where he was. Now that Ashley's life was in jeopardy who could she turn to? She pulled over and dialed a number.

"Hello, this is Louis Charles, Assistant District Attorney the Bronx, how can I help you?"

"Mr. Charles, this is Lisa Taylor, remember me?"

"Yeah. Sonny's friend, right? What can I do for you?"

"Mr. Charles, they've kidnapped Ashley, Sonny's secretary."

"Unbelievable. When did this happen?"

"What do we do? She is so sweet and innocent."

"Martinorelli will probably publicize it trying to persuade Sonny to stop assisting Stephanie. The old man isn't missing a trick is he. Lisa, let me make some calls and I will get back to you."

"In the meantime, I will try and get a location on the whereabouts of Ashley. I am really scared that they will kill her like that Police Chief. Martinorelli sounds very desperate to me. I'll talk to you soon Mr. Charles."

Ashley sat in a dark room not knowing where she was or what to do. She had fainted after being abducted and had no idea how long she was out. The two large Italian men drove her blind folded somewhere. She had no idea how far she was from the city. She thought she was going to die. She couldn't stop crying.

In the next room, the two men studied the young brunette from the other side of the two way mirror. They placed a call to Alexander advising him of their successful abduction. He was delighted.

"I want this given full publicity on the internet and television as soon as possible that Sonny Thomas' secretary is missing feared kidnapped or even murdered. This will rattle him. I will be awaiting his call any time now."

Nineteen

Dansville, New York was their next destination. They would change vehicles for the third time. Sonny thought that he did a great job on the vehicle side. He maintained his pattern of taking as many country roads as possible. Stephanie was extremely quiet for the last hour or so.

When Sonny drove through Horseheads, New York, he noticed a state trooper looking at his vehicle. Sonny drove the speed limit on the nose. The trooper put his lights on and followed them until they pulled over. Stephanie began to cry.

"Relax Steph, Martinorelli can't have everyone on his payroll. We have to play it very casual like nothing is wrong. We are still in disguise, remember."

"I know Sonny, but our photos are everywhere and have been for the last twenty-four hours. Even with the disguise we cannot hide our face."

"Just relax and breathe slowly and evenly."

The trooper remained in his vehicle and went on his computer and ran the tag on Sonny and Stephanie's vehicle, which was their third, since they left New York. After what was the longest three minutes of Sonny's life, the trooper got out of his vehicle and walked slowly to theirs.

"Evening, Sir."

"Good Evening."

"How are you today?"

"Good officer, just passing through."

"License and registration please."

Sonny had all pertinent information available and handed them to the New York State Policeman. The trooper took the license and registration back to his vehicle.

"Sonny, should we run for it? We are going to get caught."

Sonny eyed the trooper through his rear view mirror. He grabbed her hand to relax her.

"No, if he knew who we really were we would be surrounded by now by several different police agencies. Plus, these disguises are really good."

After what seemed like hours, the trooper came back to their car. He smiled at them.

"Sorry about that, we have an APB out and are stopping more vehicles than usual. A Police Chief has been murdered in Binghamton and there are two suspects that have not yet been found. Well, Mr. Kelly you have yourself a nice day."

The trooper walked back to his vehicle. As he made a U-turn driving off in the opposite direction, Sonny looked at Stephanie.

"We have to get these discs to the FBI ASAP. Our luck will not last forever."

"I am ready to pass out I am so nervous."

"At our next town we will switch cars for a fourth and final time as we are off to Dansville, New York. It is a very small town. I have done a lot of work there."

Stephanie never responded. Sonny looked at her several times. Not a movement. He pulled the car to the side of the road.

"I know we just had a close call, but what's the matter?"

She turned and looked into his eyes. The tears started to flow. She reached for him and hugged him tightly. She eventually let go and looked at him.

"What about afterwards? What am I going to do? Even if Alexander is arrested, a trial could take years. Where will I go? With all the power he has my life will be in jeopardy even if he is arrested."

She continued to cry gently, facing out the passenger window. Sonny inched closer to her and embraced her lovingly.

"I know you can't see it now, but this will be over before you know it. Hopefully, by tomorrow. Alexander will be where he belongs, Federal prison. Then you can start a new life with me. Please say yes to me this time. I never stopped loving you even though we were separated. I want to marry you, Steph."

"Promise?"

"Absolutely."

The two hugged and kissed before Sonny said no time for this. Yet. They proceeded to drive towards Dansville, New York. Both held hands and for the moment were happy.

Twenty

"Hello, this is Special Agent Jeffers, how can I help you?"

"Hello, Agent Jeffers, this is Assistant District Attorney, Louis Charles. I had a message that you want to meet with me, sir."

"Yes I do. Mr. Charles, is there any way we can meet today? I have to get as much information on Sonny Thomas and Stephanie Martinorelli as I can. I know Stephanie was reported missing, but they both were spotted in Binghamton, New York. They are both the prime suspects in the murder of New York City Police Chief Roger Fordrani, last night."

"Yeah, I heard. I don't believe a word of it though. Sounds like a Martinorelli tactic to get his discs back ASAP. I am certain you know that Sonny's secretary has been kidnapped most likely by Martinorelli."

" I did and we have several agents working on it as we speak. Now you were, I understand, the third member of their Law School study group? You also were very close with both of them. Let's meet at Annie's Diner in White Plains. Not too far, is it?"

"I'll be there within an hour."

C.J. Jeffers just finished his first cup of coffee and was waiting on a second when Louis Charles walked into the diner. The two men shook each others hand.

"Sorry, tough time of day to get a cab."

The two men sat down and ordered their meals. Once they ordered they spoke non-stop.

"Thanks for meeting me at a moment's notice, Mr Charles."

"No problem, Sonny and Stephanie mean a lot to me."

"Why would Sonny jeopardize everything for Stephanie?"

"You get right to the point don't you Special Agent. I don't think even Sonny knows that it was common knowledge by most of the Law School that these two had a thing for each other. When they basically left a party not returning until graduation, the matter seemed closed that they would end up together. My gut instinct, being around them so much, was that they had mutual love for each other. It wasn't consummated, I guess, until those last couple of days of Law School. To this day Sonny never spoke to me about it. After we graduated, for some reason, they went their separate ways – until now that is."

"Interesting. Did Sonny ever tell you what Stephanie had in her possession that Alexander Martinorelli so desperately wants?"

"Yes, he did."

"What is in her possession?"

"Stephanie somehow came into possession of **Twelve Discs** that include Alexander Martinorelli's licit and illicit nationwide personnel and payroll. I reviewed the **Twelve Discs** with Sonny at our Alma Mater Law School library. The names on these discs will blow your mind."

Lou drank his coffee until it was bottomless. He motioned with his cup to his waitress that he would like another. Jeffers could not hide his excitement at hearing this.

"Oh, one other thing Special Agent Jeffers, the old man is a member of the *Commission* which has exponentially transformed from solely a criminal empire hierarchy to the status of leading businessmen in the world. World bankers, politicians, members of the tri-lateral commission and the builderberg group make up this group. I have never witnessed such power in one *Commission*. They are placed in strategic leadership positions throughout the United States. To be a member you have to be the elite of the elite in money and power."

Lou then excused himself as he had to visit the men's room. When he returned, he took a gulp of coffee and said,

"After Sonny and I reviewed the discs, I did a more complete background on the old man and advised Sonny to totally avoid this matter of assisting Stephanie. He flatly refused. He said he would get Martinorelli first."

The two meals arrived and the two men ate them quickly. C.J. Jeffers had a thousand questions, he just did not know where to start.

"Charles, you have known Sonny for some time. How do you think he'll play this out?"

"Well, I think safety will be a priority, Stephanie's that is. Sir, Sonny knows the State of New York pretty good. His investigation company worked the entire state. He once told me that if he was ever on the run, that he could hide for years in New York. Upstate, Central and Western New York were ideal locations due to all of the small towns and country roads. A New York run would be ideal for him now."

C.J.Jeffers stroked his goatee. He took another swig of his coffee. He looked directly into Louis Charles eyes.

"So, you think he is in New York still?

"Yes. My bet is that he already tried to contact an honest FBI Special Agent."

Jeffers looked down. When he looked up Lou Charles was gazing at him.

"He already did, didn't he sir?"

"Well, I did get the information rather quickly."

"Special Agent Jeffers, Sonny knows what is at stake. He knows how far Martinorelli 's influence extends in the criminal, political and business worlds."

"Charles, I think he might contact you. Who else can he possibly trust at this point? When he contacts you advise him that the FBI is sending special agents by the dozens throughout New York to assist him. You tell him, starting with me, that we are on his side. Give him my name and my personal cell phone number. You understand?"

C.J. Jeffers was very excited at this point. He got up, walked around the table and sat next to Louis Charles. Face to face. His passion now was overflowing.

"You tell him the FBI wants Alexander Martinorelli, and, based on what you said about the **Twelve Discs'** that is all that we will need to conduct a thorough investigation into the criminal element and finally give the old man what he deserves. A final visit to the Federal Penitentiary."

"I can do that."

"Charles, be careful. He is a dangerous man with a lot of connections."

"Don't worry about me, sir. Get to Sonny and Stephanie before it's too late."

The two men shook hands and exchanged personal cell phone numbers. The meeting had been a success. Both men were satisfied. They would never see each other alive, ever again.

Twenty One

Sonny and Stephanie arrived in Dansville, New York. They registered at the Dansville Inn, located in the center of the small town. They unpacked and laid down on the king bed.

"I hope that phone call this morning gets to the right special agent."

"It will. When you toss around a name as powerful as Alexander Martinorelli along with the accusations you made, well, some special agent will respond."

"Yeah, you're right, but how do we know it wasn't overheard by someone on the old man's payroll?"

"We don't, but at a minimum two special agents will know about your phone call this morning."

Sonny reached over and kissed Stephanie on the lips. Then he hugged her.

"I forgot how you always know the right thing to say to me."

"Probably because of all those hours studying the Law together. I'm a little hungry, can you go grab some snacks? I won't move. I promise. The store is walking distance away. "

"I'll be right back. *Do not* leave the motel."

" Yes sir."

"This is Special Agent C.J. Jeffers, how can I help you?"

"Sir, this is Louis Charles."

"Yeah, we just left each others company an hour ago. What is it?"

"Any updates on the whereabouts of Sonny Thomas' secretary Ashley. I have had zero luck so far."

C.J. Jeffers stood up and walked around his desk a few times. As he sat again, he was shaking his head. Nothing yet, I hate those words he thought.

"Charles, let me check with our surveillance people. Maybe she was caught on tape. Nevertheless, as I indicated at the diner, now is the time Sonny will try to get a hold of you. Keep in mind that any phone call may be bugged, so speak in generalities. Do not ask his present location. Just as a precaution."

"OK, I will get back to you when I hear something."

C.J. Jeffers poured himself another cup of coffee. Looking down at the busy streets of New York City he wished he was closer to Sonny and Stephanie. In the last twenty-four hours, Sonny and Stephanie have become chief suspects in the murder of a New York City Police Chief. Now the secretary of Sonny Thomas has been kidnapped most likely by the Martinorelli organization. He thought we must get those discs before Martinorelli gets to Sonny and Stephanie. Everything has Martinorelli's fingerprints on it, the murder, the kidnapping. He dialed his desk phone.

"Huntington."

"Yes sir."

"Martinorelli is not himself. He is panicking that Sonny and Stephanie will get the discs to the FBI before he can get to them. Murder and now kidnapping are high risk crimes and does not sound like the old man. His personality would never risk what he is presently doing. Maybe he is not as smart as he thinks he is. There is always a danger when you think you are the smartest guy in the room. These recent crimes cannot be his only criminal activity. Do an extensive search regarding any unsolved criminal activity during his reign as boss. If he is this desperate now he must have some culpability for something in his past. I want Martinorelli for the Fordrani murder and the kidnapping. The old man is slipping and I am going to get him."

Twenty Two

"Here, I stopped and picked up a few snacks. It is getting too dangerous so I bought some for travel. The more we are out of anyone's view, the better."

Sonny turned and looked at Stephanie who was pale. He quickly walked over to her.

"Steph, what's wrong?"

"I went on my Smart Phone and, well, they have kidnapped your secretary, Ashley."

Sonny put the snacks down on the bed. He then proceeded to hug Stephanie. He could not believe Martinorelli would resort to kidnapping.

"It's all my fault, Sonny. I never should have gotten you involved with this. Ashley would never have been kidnapped, but for me. Should we just send the discs back to him and run away?"

"No! Although the running away part sounds nice, I have to see what is going on. First, the murder in Binghamton and now this. Martinorelli does not want us to get these discs to the FBI. Let me make a call."

"Good evening, this is Louis Charles, Bronx District Attorney Office. How can I help you?"

"Lou, it's me, Sonny. What is going on? Now they have kidnapped Ashley?"

"Sonny, Martinorelli does not want those discs to get to the FBI. I have been in contact with a Special Agent from the FBI, C.J. Jeffers. He anticipated that you would call me. Take down his cell phone number. This Special Agent wants Martinorelli more than you and Stephanie. He personally told me to tell you that he is on your side. He does not think you had anything to do with the murder of the Police Chief in Binghamton."

"I don't know, Lou. Let me think about it. Are you certain this Special Agent Jeffers is legitimate and not on the old man's payroll? I mean he has a nationwide payroll. We both saw it at the Law School. Those discs will ruin him and he knows it."

"Gut instinct, not a chance. You should have seen his eyes when I told him Stephanie had Alexander Martinorelli's discs."

"Why would Martinorelli murder someone on his own payroll? He expeditiously wants to implicate us."

"He is desperate and based on the last couple of days he will stop at nothing to stop you. I feel you should contact Special Agent, C.J. Jeffers as soon as you can."

"Lou, I'll think about it. I guess it wouldn't hurt to call him. My phone is untraceable. Thanks for all of your help."

Sonny hung up his Smart Phone. Maybe Lou is right and Special Agent Jeffers is an honest FBI man. Curiously, Lou never mentioned his own District Attorney's office. That meant there were attorney's there on the Martinorelli payroll.

It was late and Lou Charles decided to call it a day. He worked late almost every day. It was dark as he walked to his vehicle. He was thinking of Sonny and Stephanie. He was worried. He knew how much power Alexander Martinorelli had, but the FBI special agent gave him hope that they would succeed.

Louis Charles smiled to himself. After talking to his "buddy" Sonny Thomas, he was glad he was able to give him C.J. Jeffers cell phone number. With all that had happened the last couple of days, it seemed that Martinorelli was getting closer to being indicted because of the discs in Sonny and Stephanie's possession. He knew how stubborn Sonny was, and he also knew his buddy would contact C.J. Jeffers when he thought the time was right.

He never noticed the black limousine a block and a half behind him. Michael Martinorelli and Petey Mancini watched Louis Charles enter his vehicle. Louis Charles turned on the ignition and never felt a thing as his vehicle exploded, rising ten feet in the air. He died instantly.

Michael Martinorelli smiled and turned to the driver of the black limousine, Petey Mancini, and said,

"Good job Petey. Now let's get out of here. He won't be helping his friends anymore."

Twenty Three

Jimmy Degregorio arrived in Dansville, New York shortly after dusk. He registered in a national franchise hotel for the evening. Jimmy D laid his suitcase on the double bed. He proceeded to pull out photos of Sonny Thomas and Stephanie Martinorelli. From the lips of Alexander Martinorelli, he was ordered to eliminate the pair and return the discs to their owner. Piece of cake, he thought to himself. All he had to do was find them. They would never be able to avoid Jimmy D and his knife. He looked forward to life in the legitimate corporate world of Alexander Martinorelli.

Alexander Martinorelli sat at his desk with his arms folded. His attorney, Charles Stefano, read him the riot act about all of the publicity that he was getting with this Sonny Thomas thing going on. He never answered just listened to his personal attorney.

"Alex, you have to relax and run your organization like you always have. Silent. Two murders and a kidnapping is all over the internet and TV. Your face is connected to everything that mentions your daughter-in-law and that private investigator. You have to insulate yourself from those two for the time being. Guilt by association is powerful. "

"Charles, my friend, I know how loyal you are, but every part of my world, including you, is on those discs. The *Commission* would have to act and most likely not in my favor. I must get those discs or it is all over."

Charles walked around the office not knowing what to tell his oldest client. He stood directly in front of his client.

"Alex with the murders of Roger Fordrani and Louis Charles accompanied with the kidnapping of the private investigator's secretary there is a direct link to the disappearance of Stephanie. You are a prime suspect. The FBI would never deduce these crimes to be a mere coincidence. Your fingerprints are all over this."

"I don't know Charles. If we do not get them before the FBI my entire organization may be lost. A lifetime of building an impenetrable organization. Being one of only 36 members of the *Commission*. All lost because of them."

"I understand Alex. I understand all you can lose. Myself included as I am on your payroll; however, in the interim, we should take some precautions and prepare a plan in the event the discs fall into the hands of the FBI."

He stared out of his window for a few minutes, Alexander turned to his trusted old friend. He knew that he was right. Begrudgingly, Alexander nodded and Charles Stefano walked out of his office. This was new to him. He never had to plan on being caught by anyone.

Twenty Four

Sonny and Stephanie looked blankly at their Smart Phones. The special news bulletin on their e-mail reported that Louis Charles, Assistant District Attorney of the Bronx Office in New York, was killed as his vehicle was car bombed. A complete investigation is under way. Sonny could not believe what he just read. Stephanie started to cry. Sonny walked back and forth, tears in his eyes. What did I do to my buddy he thought. He stood up and looked at Stephanie.

"The Bronx District Attorney's Office must have been bugged by Martinorelli and his people. All Lou did, as far as they knew, was talk once on the phone to me. One time!"

"Sonny they must have found out how close the three of us really were. Lou would have done anything to help us. He did not realize the danger that he was in."

Stephanie started to cry a little harder this time. Sonny grabbed and held her. He began to quietly sob for his buddy.

_____

Jimmy D had driven for a few hours in Dansville, New York trying to locate Sonny and Stephanie. He would try for a little longer he thought. If he found nothing, he would report to Rocco and leave tomorrow morning and head west bound.

Jimmy checked all of the local and national hotels and their registrations, but there was no sign of them. He decided to check a couple of motels on Main Street. While slowly driving, he did notice one car parked in the parking lot of the Dansville Inn. No one else appeared to be at the motel. He thought that he would give it a shot.

"Good evening ma'am, my name is Jimmy and I was wondering if you could help me find my brother and his wife."

Dottie, the motel manager, not knowing any better said,

"The only couple we have is in Room 7, but I don't know if they are married."

After Dottie refused to allow Jimmy D to view the registration, he thanked Dottie anyway. He left and drove two blocks away and parked in the parking lot of Livingston Mutual Insurance Company. He caressed his knife, put on his gloves and headed to the Dansville Inn, Room 7.

I think we should leave now. If Martinorelli can commit two murders within two days, he must have all his bulls out after us."

"OK, Sonny. I'll start packing."

"I'll go check us out now then."

Jimmy D saw the room door close and observed Sonny walk and enter the motel office. Jimmy D quickly ran over to Room 7 and knocked lightly.

"Why are you knocking, Sonny?"

Jimmy D burst into the room and Stephanie screamed.

"I will take those discs now Stephanie, you shouldn't take things that don't belong to you."

Jimmy D pulled out his knife and inched closer and closer to her. Stephanie backed up, not knowing what to do.

"Look, give me the discs and I'll make your death as painless as I can. What do you think? You cannot beat a man like Alexander Martinorelli. Come on give me the discs and I will make it quick."

He kept moving so slow. He knew she had no escape route. Suddenly, when he thought he was close enough to her, he went to grab her. While in motion forward, Stephanie gave him a roundhouse kick that caught his nose flush, easily breaking it, knocking him down. Embarrassed, Jimmy D rushed at her again, knife first. Stephanie ripped the old fashioned telephone from the wall and hit Jimmy D on his head just as he was almost on her. He now laid on the floor unconscious. She took his infamous knife.

Sonny rushed in and could not believe what he saw. Stephanie sitting on the king bed with a knife pointed at the head of the now unconscious Jimmy D.

"Steph, how did you... What did you... Are you okay?"

Stephanie cried and while her whole body was shaking said,

"Yeah, I think we should get out of here."

Within minutes Sonny and Stephanie were driving westbound on Route 81. Destination Buffalo, New York. From the highway the two observed the number of different police agencies at the motel, and the myriad of lights and sirens.

"This is Special Agent Jeffers, how can I help you?"

"Sir, this is Huntington. There was an arrest literally minutes ago in Dansville, New York. An alleged associate of Alexander Martinorelli was tied to a bedpost with a note attached to him. It said he was a hired gun for the Martinorelli organization. His nose was badly broken and he suffered a concussion. The note went on and explained his ordered hit was on both Sonny Thomas and Stephanie Martinorelli."

"Huntington, this sounds like Sonny Thomas to me."

C.J. Jeffers thought as Huntington had put his phone down. It will be nearly impossible to get Martinorelli on the hearsay evidence on this note. Huntington returned.

"Evan, even though we know the contract with Martinorelli is most likely true, let's try and keep a low profile on this arrest if possible in this Twitter, Facebook age that we live in. There is no need to draw any more attention to the whereabouts of Sonny and Stephanie."

Twenty Five

After hearing about the death of Louis Charles, Lisa Taylor became even more anxious to find the whereabouts of Ashley. Although an expert in the location of missing persons, and a former police officer, she did not have any luck so far. She had to move quickly.

"Yes, can I please speak with Special Agent, C.J. Jeffers?"

After waiting approximately two and a half minutes,

"This is Special Agent Jeffers."

"Sir, my name is Lisa Taylor, I spoke with District Attorney Louis Charles about a recent kidnapping. Now I find out that he was murdered. What is going on sir?"

"We are working on it Ms. Taylor. I was very sorry to hear about Charles, I had just met with him. He was helping the FBI with this Martinorelli thing."

"Special Agent Jeffers, we have to find Ashley. These two murders were already committed most likely in an effort to stop Sonny and Stephanie. An additional murder would mean nothing to the Martinorelli organization, if it would get Sonny and Stephanie quicker."

"We are doing what we can Ms. Taylor. We have a ton of surveillance on everything the old man owns."

"Please keep me posted. I think her time is limited. "

"I will ma'am."

The internet and evening newscasts ran steady story lines on Sonny Thomas and Stephanie Martinorelli. CNN, MSNBC, FOX NEWS, CBS, NBC, and ABC all ran stories on the situation. Accusations that they were responsible for the death of police chief Fordrani were fueled by people on the Martinorelli payroll. It was national news. Every station was talking about Sonny and Stephanie. Now with the death of Louis Charles and the kidnapping of Thomas' secretary, the story lines increasingly included Alexander Martinorelli.

In Newark, New Jersey, the *Commission* met. This matter regarding Alexander Martinorelli and the other two individuals on the run caused great concern among the seated twenty-seven of the thirty-six members.

The *Commission* had been around almost a century. Their members were of such a high profile and power that they always won. Their mission was to govern the affairs of not only the entire crime syndicate, but also govern political and business affairs on a nationwide scale.

The *Commission*, composed of thirty-six members, would function as both a judiciary and a legislature. It would adjudicate disputes nationwide and vote on matters of overall policy. Over the years the *Commission* evolved into a business equal to the largest corporations combined.

Memorandums had been handed out to the twenty-seven members of the *Commission*. The members dined, ate world famous liquors and drank coffee. At the conclusion of the festive meal, one of the Upper Elite Board Member stood. Applause filled the meeting room.

"Gentleman, thank you all for attending this meeting on such short notice. While I realize we all have our obligations to the *Commission*, I am grateful. Nonetheless, one of our members, Alexander Martinorelli, one of our most popular and experienced members, has put himself in a situation that if he fails to remedy we as a *Commission* must act. The negligence exhibited to permit such critical information to become public is inexcusable. Any possible implication of any of the present membership is unforgivable, I feel, and we will vote on it as is our custom. If this information makes it to the FBI we as a

Commission have to personally take care of our member, Alexander Martinorelli. While we all have loyalty among ourselves, our primary loyalty is to the *Commission*."

The esteemed member sat down and the room lit up with conversation. There was some emotion being exhibited in the room. Alexander Martinorelli had been with the *Commission* for over forty years. After fifteen minutes of deliberation and heated discussions, the *Commission* had made their decision.

Twenty Six

As soon as he could Sonny exited off Route 81 and changed to Route 20, a more country and less congested county road. The situation back in Dansville was way too close for comfort for Sonny. He did recall now that Stephanie had a black belt, but he somehow forgot that until now. It was dark and he was traveling westbound. Final destination: Buffalo, New York.

"I think I'm spooked enough now to try that Special Agent, Jeffers tomorrow. These discs have been copied. I have to let him know how I will get the originals to him. The copies won't hold up in court due to evidentiary issues. Lou was positive that he was an honest Federal Agent."

"Sonny, whatever you think. I just want this to end. I was terrified back there."

" You handled it perfectly, Darling."

Sonny drove staring straight ahead into the darkness. He was still feeling fortunate that Stephanie handled that associate like she did. He looked at her. She was everything he wanted. Everything so far had worked out. He was still uncertain how to get in touch with the honest FBI Agent, though.

"Steph, I know that I have to get in contact with Jeffers. I am not certain how to do it. Any thoughts?"

Stephanie told Sonny what she thought would be foolproof. He listened to her.

"Okay, sounds good to me. I have his personal cell phone. I will try him tomorrow morning."

Salvatore Puzero had reviewed his instructions regarding Sonny Thomas and Stephanie Martinorelli, but he was growing impatient. He paced back and forth in his motel room. He was in Ithaca, New York. His cell phone rang,

"Salvatore, it's Tony, Sonny Thomas and Stephanie Martinorelli were last spotted in Dansville, New York about an hour ago. While we are unsure, we think they are heading westbound. Check the side roads. No clue of them on the I-90 as of yet."

"I'm on my way."

"Oh. One other thing..."

"What?"

"Jimmy D was pinched in Dansville. The FBI arrived first because of an anonymous phone call. He was arrested at a motel. He had a handwritten note attached to his chest that indicated he was a hired hit man with orders from Alexander Martinorelli to terminate Sonny and Stephanie. You believe the nerve of those two? They are suicidal."

Salvatore Puzero said nothing and ended the call.

Michael Martinorelli and Petey Mancini sped westbound on Route I-90 after hearing that Sonny and Stephanie were allegedly now in or not far from Dansville, New York.

"I've have to get them Petey, or I'm probably a dead man, regardless of who my father is. I have to make up for the mistake of a lifetime. I have to get Stephanie. That would be justice."

Petey Mancini said nothing in response and kept driving twenty miles over the speed limit. If for some reason the discs were handed over to the FBI before they could get them, he was uncertain what, if any, future Michael Martinorelli had. It did not matter to him, he did not make decisions, never did. He carried out orders plain and simple. It did not matter to him what they were. His loyalty has been, always will be, to his boss, Alexander Martinorelli. Petey teared up thinking about his boss.

"I cannot believe Petey this entire organization may be ruined because of my negligence of those damned discs. I will get her or them or I will die trying."

Twenty Seven

It was late and C.J. Jeffers sat behind his desk with both hands on his chin. How could he put more pressure on Alexander Martinorelli? He most likely is responsible for the murder of a New York City Police Chief. He most likely is responsible for the kidnapping of Sonny Thomas' secretary. He most likely ordered the murder of Louis Charles, an Assistant District Attorney and, close friend of Sonny Thomas and Stephanie Martinorelli. I just sit here and do nothing about it. I just have to rile him up. A thought just occurred to the Special Agent.

"Huntington."

The Special Agent hurried into Jeffers office and closed the door. He stood there and looked at his superior.

"I am sick and tired of waiting. Tomorrow, I want to put pressure on Alexander Martinorelli, like he's never had before in his life. He has gone too far the last couple of days. I want twenty-five of his top employees arrested tomorrow before they leave for work. Cite some fraudulent misrepresentation, which most likely is true, and bring them all here. Embarrass them. Do not let them even change clothes. Treat them like convicted criminals which they soon will be."

"On it, sir."

"Also, get in touch with Lisa Taylor, she may be in danger because of her relationship with Sonny."

Salvatore Puzero continued driving westbound on Route 20. His stoic face never changed as he drove above the posted speed limit. He had decided to take the side roads. He believed Thomas was avoiding the I-90 and Route 81 intentionally. He was as deranged as any associate on Martinorelli's payroll. He actually liked committing murder. It showed him how powerful and superior he was compared to everyone else. He would get them himself.

"Well, hopefully that note will raise more suspicion on the old man. His name should start to appear online and in the newspapers as much as ours are now. Of course, on the other hand, it could make him more desperate to get us."

"He will stop at nothing to save his organization, Sonny. Even if Alexander is arrested, won't it take years before he is tried?"

"With New York's Speedy Trial Statutes, it should probably take a year. Of course, he will be incarcerated during that year. That my dear is a way off anyway, we must get these original discs to Special Agent, Jeffers."

Sonny continued to drive. Stephanie snuggled next to him holding him tightly. He grabbed the back of her neck and massaged it because she loved it. This will be over soon he thought. He hoped.

"About thirty miles and we will be in Batavia. There is an excellent doughnut shop right on the way. I could use some coffee."

"Me too."

"It just occurred to me that this *Commission* that Alexander is a member of cannot be too pleased with the publicity that the old man is getting. For over forty years he has been a powerful figure. Now, because we have possession of the discs, he has acted out of character. The murders, the kidnapping, forget the FBI, the *Commission*, may beat everyone to him."

Stephanie just looked at the countryside as Sonny spoke. Her entire life would be changed because of these discs. One thing she knew for certain and it grew stronger every minute she was with him. She was madly in love with Sonny Thomas.

Twenty Eight

Earlier as Sonny and Stephanie were leaving Dansville, Lisa Taylor could not stop thinking about how she could find Ashley. She also wondered where Sonny and Stephanie were. She admitted to herself that she was jealous of Stephanie. She knew that she had to find Ashley before Sonny turned the discs over to the FBI, Ashley's life depended on it.

Throughout the day she checked some of the property owned by Alexander Martinorelli. Houses, condominiums, town houses and offices were scattered everywhere in New York and even in Europe. Lisa telephoned Special Agent, C. J. Jeffers.

"This is Special Agent Jeffers, how can I help you?"

"Hi sir, it's Lisa Taylor, again. I apologize for calling so late."

"No problem. I'm still here. I do have some interesting news for you about Martinorelli."

"What, I have to find Ashley tonight. He'll never let her live if the discs are in the hands of the FBI."

"Well, I was going to call you first thing tomorrow. It seems our surveillance was pretty intense. Ten separate locations were under surveillance twenty-four-seven.

These locations were either owned or controlled by Alexander Martinorelli. We caught some interesting surveillance from earlier yesterday, right around the time that Ashley was kidnapped. The location was one of his cabins."

"Where is the cabin located? I'll go right now!"

"Well, Miss Taylor, Alexander has a summer cottage a couple of miles from the Hudson River in White Plains, New York. Our surveillance team observed two large men in overcoats holding a third unidentified individual. The tape fails to depict if this person is a small man or average sized woman. I am planning on sending a team of special agents first thing in the morning."

"Sir, what is the address?"

"Look, Miss Taylor, I would rather you let the FBI take care of this. It could be dangerous."

"Please Special Agent Jeffers, if someone does not get to her tonight there may not be a tomorrow for her. The address, please."

"On one condition, you go with a team of special agent's tomorrow morning."

"Deal," *she Lied*.

"OK, remember nothing until you meet up with the special agents. The cottage is located at 513282 Brooklyn Drive, White Plains, New York."

"I'll have the team of special agents contact you where you can meet them tomorrow."

"Sorry sir, can't wait."

Lisa shut off her phone, C.J. Jeffers punched his desk. He should have known better. He dialed his cell phone.

"Vincent Daniello, Special Agent, how can I help you?"

"Daniello, I have an emergency situation here."

"Shoot, sir."

"Remember the kidnapping of Sonny Thomas' secretary yesterday?"

"Yes sir. We have been working on it all day."

"I want you and a team, rather a couple of teams, to go to the cottage caught on surveillance. I was going to wait until tomorrow morning, but I told the other private investigator, Lisa Taylor, the address. I should not have. She most likely is on her way there right now. It is dangerous, but she couldn't wait. It is far too dangerous for her alone. Get there as fast as you can and report back to me."

"I am on it sir."

Vincent Daniello called his partner, Chris Hyman and relayed the information. They both contacted the other teams of agents and headed towards the cottage.

"Let's go Chris. We have to fly, she has a head start on us."

"Vince, it's going to be a long night, better stop and get some coffee on the way."

Twenty Nine

It took over an hour, but she found it. The cottage was secluded from the other cottages. Lisa Taylor drove past the cottage in a pre-surveillance fashion. She hoped her days as a police officer and now a private investigator would help her now. Ashley's life depended on it.

Parked in the driveway of the cottage was a black limousine. She drove a block away and parked her vehicle in a newly cemented driveway where some new construction was being completed. It was dark and she could barely see in front of her. Preparation was always her focus so she loaded her 38 as she walked toward the cottage. She brought some mace. Couldn't hurt she thought. Lisa knew her chances would increase if she was somehow able to catch the Martinorelli associates off their guard. She was, at this point, uncertain how many of Martinorelli men were even in the cabin. Maybe she should have listened to Special Agent Jeffers and wait for the FBI. No way she thought. She was not even certain that Ashley was there.

Lisa inched her way toward the cabin. She was determined to save Ashley. She approached the driveway and peered inside from a side window.

What she observed was two large Italian men playing cards, drinking and smoking cigars. When do these guys sleep she thought? It was the middle of the night. The two men were focused on their card game, and occasionally they laughed. The room was inundated with cigar smoke.

Lisa walked around the entire cabin, but did not see any sign of Ashley. Her immediate plan was to get the two large men out of the cabin. Then she at least would have a chance she thought. She had a feeling that Ashley had to be saved tonight. Setting off the limousine's alarm was relatively easy.

When the two men heard the loud annoying sound they ran out of the cabin yelling profanities every step of the way.

Lisa rushed into the cabin through the side kitchen door. The two men turned the alarm off. They then re-entered the cabin. Lisa walked down the dark corridor. There were a row of doors on each side of the corridor. She crept trying to not make a sound. First one on the left - empty. First one on the right - empty.

"Maybe you should check on our hostage."

"No problem."

Lisa continued down the corridor. The second door on the left – BINGO. A tied up Ashley had electrical tape over her mouth and both arms tied up with tape behind her back. Ashley's eyes opened wide and tears of joy fell down her cheeks. Lisa put her finger to her mouth. She gently closed the door.

Within thirty seconds the large man entered the room. He smiled as he approached Ashley. Lisa came from behind and struck the back of the large man's head with a ten pound paper weight that she found in the room. The large man fell to the floor knocking him unconscious. The fall caused a loud thump.

Hearing the loud thump, the other large man took out his 38 and walked down the dark corridor.

Special Agents, Vincent Daniello and Chris Hyman, parked their vehicle a block from the cabin. It was 2 blocks from where Lisa parked her vehicle. As they approached the cabin, they observed the black limousine parked in the cabin driveway. They spoke on cell phones to the other seven parties of FBI Agents. They were uncertain where Lisa was, but they were fairly certain she was there.

The large man opened the door and viewed his companion lying on the floor face down. There was no sign of Ashley who somehow must have got loose through the large man. He turned around and turned on the light. Nothing. No one was there. Lisa drew her thirty-eight and said,

"Drop it, or you're a dead man."

The man turned around and saw Lisa. He started to laugh.

"What do you think you're doing young lady?" Give me the gun and no one gets hurt."

Lisa shot the man's left knee cap and he started to scream in pain. She smiled at him pointing her gun at his other knee.

"You going to drop it now tough guy? From the looks of it, you only have one good knee left."

The large man obliged. He tossed his revolver on the floor and pushed it with his right foot to her. He wanted to kill her.

"Thank you. Now that was not hard was it."

She continued to smile at the associate. In a lot of pain now, the large man listened to Lisa's further instruction to turn around and put his arms behind his back. As Lisa was almost done handcuffing him, headlights appeared in the window. This startled both of them. The large man turned around and caught Lisa off-guard. He rushed her and Lisa fired another shot out of desperation.

Outside, four other associates of Alexander Martinorelli exited their limousine.

"Hey, what was that?" yelled one of the newly arrived associates.

The four men charged into the cabin. They heard the large man yell to them. When they arrived in the room, he had Lisa in a choke hold. He had managed to get her 38. Unbeknownst to the new arrivals, Ashley was hiding under a desk at the very end of the corridor.

"What the hell happened here?"

"She tried to rescue the secretary, but I got her first."

The four men looked at the left knee of the large man.

"Who got who first? Speaking of the secretary, where is she?"

"I don't know. I've been busy. She can't be too far."

Ashley nervously sat as still as she could. She heard the four associates searching every room in the cabin. She thought that she should make a run for it and try to get out of the window. She was very frightened and could not move. What should she do? One of the associates walked toward the room that she was in.

He opened the door and noticed that the window was open. He ran to the window and looked out into the darkness. He saw nothing but black.

Ashley was running as fast as she ever had in her life. She fell several times before she ran right into the arms of a man. She screamed at the top of her lungs.

Vincent Daniello held her.

"Hey, don't worry. It's the FBI, you're safe."

"Lisa Taylor is still in there. Some new associates just arrived. Please help her, she saved my life! Please hurry."

"Don't worry ma'am. We'll make sure she is OK."

Daniello called the other special agents who were within minutes of being at the cabin. He gave his orders and they all waited.

Inside the cabin the large man pointed his 38 at Lisa. She smugly refused to show any emotion, even though she had never been more afraid in her life.

"Tell me where she is. I'll make your death as painless as I can."

The other four associates heard the multiple car doors slamming outside. One of them ran to the window.

"Boss, there are a bunch of feds out there. What do we do?"

Over a loud speaker Vincent Daniello said:

"Release Lisa Taylor now or there won't be much of a cabin left for your boss. You have exactly 2 minutes or we start shooting."

The four men discussed their options. When the large man refused to let her go they overruled him.

"Look, we don't have a chance of getting out of here alive. Let her go, now. The Boss will figure a way to get us out of this. He always does. "

Within a minute Lisa Taylor walked out of the cabin safe and sound. When Ashley saw Lisa, she ran to her and hugged her. Both women were overcome with emotion. Both wiped each others tears from their respective faces.

"Thank you so much Lisa. You are the bravest person I have ever met. I don't know how you knew where I was. Thank You so much."

"Well, the FBI helped with finding your location. I just had to figure how to get you out of there tonight. I just could not imagine you being held hostage. I knew that time was running out."

The six associates of Martinorelli were handcuffed and placed under arrest by the myriad of FBI special agents. The one large man held an ice pack on his head. The other large man was taken away by ambulance, his left knee would never be the same.

Vincent Daniello smiled at the two women. He reported to Jeffers that they had the hostage and she was safe. Jeffers was obviously thrilled to hear the news.

"Ashley, you have to come with me and Chris. Federal Regulations mandate that you have to be examined by a physician and a psychologist. We will take you to our hospital, OK?"

"No problem, sir."

Ashley ran to Lisa again, and gave her a big bear hug. She entered the special agent's vehicle. Lisa was not done, yet. She drove **_westbound towards Western New York._**

Thirty

Sonny Thomas pulled into the local doughnut shop in Batavia, New York. It was still dark. It was the middle of the night. The two of them entered the doughnut shop and sat down. The only employee, a middle aged woman, at the shop came to their table.

" How can I help you two this morning?"

"We'll have two coffees and two cinnamon raisin bagels."

Surreptitiously, Salvatore Puzero was on their tail. He spotted them just outside of Batavia. He parked a block and a half away from the doughnut shop. He was correct when he felt that Sonny was taking only side roads, avoiding the major routes. He would wait and at the most opportune moment he would get the discs. He sat behind the wheel and glared at the doughnut shop.

"I am glad that Lou told us about C.J. Jeffers. After we leave here let's go grab a motel and get a few hours of sleep. I am totally exhausted. Tomorrow is a big day. Finally, I can see a light at the end of the tunnel."

"I still feel nervous, Sonny. Michael will come after us with everything he has. He will come after me personally, I know it."

"He will have to get by me, sweetie. Once I get these original discs to the FBI it will be a matter of time before this is over. We just have to avoid Martinorelli and whoever he sends after us. He must be beyond desperate at this point."

Salvatore Puzero was an assassin. He was born and raised in New York and became a thug early on in his life. His temper was violent and his overall personality was sociopathic. He watched their vehicle waiting for the right moment. His patience was incredible. He knew he had them.

"Well, what do you think?"

"About what, Sonny?"

"Let's go."

Just then, two New York State Troopers walked into the doughnut shop. One of the troopers stopped and eyed Sonny and Stephanie, who were still in disguise. The trooper looked at his Smart Phone and then at the two of them. He proceeded to sit down and looked away.

"Yeah, I'm finished. Let's go."

The two slowly walked to their vehicle. Neither looked back at the doughnut shop. They drove away. Both looked at each other and sighed together.

Salvatore Puzero could not surprise the two of them now. He stepped on the gas and followed Sonny and Stephanie at a safe distance behind so as not to arouse any suspicion. He punched his dashboard.

Petey Mancini drove Westbound on the I-90 toward Buffalo, New York. It was very early in the morning with a couple of hours of night fall left. After the Jimmy Degregorio situation in Dansville, the organization was furious over the note that was left. Ten different vehicles were behind Petey and Michael. Alexander wanted Sonny and Stephanie within twenty-four hours or else heads would roll. With Alexander this was not a figure of speech.

"Hey, Petey, how long until we arrive in Buffalo?"

"Three hours or less."

"I'm going to try and sleep a little, if you don't mind."

"Get your rest, we're going to need it tomorrow."

———————————

Sonny took Route 20 from Batavia. The roads were very empty, which worked for Sonny. Within an hour he arrived just outside of Buffalo, New York. He turned into the Orchard Park motel in a suburb of Buffalo. It was still dark.

"Steph, I have to sleep a few hours. I'm dying here."

"Me too. We are going to need plenty of energy for tomorrow."

Sonny checked in with the hotel manager. They went inside and were asleep almost immediately.

Salvatore Puzero was still on their tail. He observed them turn into the motel. He drove past the motel. He would visit them tomorrow. They would make a mistake, he knew it and felt it. He smiled eerily into the rear view mirror. Salvatore did a U-turn and returned to the Orchard Park Motel and registered as a guest. He would not make the same mistake that Jimmy D did earlier. He had his own unique plan.

Thirty One

By 6:00 am twenty five employees of Alexander Martinorelli's business world were in custody at the New York City FBI headquarters. The threats, the complaining, every other word mentioned lawsuit was prevalent in the holding tank. These employees included bank presidents, judges, and insurance executives, among the members affiliated with the Martinorelli organization. These employees, as high level as they were, were embarrassed beyond belief. To make matters worse, the special agents would not let them get out of their pajamas.

Alexander's cell phone rang. He was at his residence having a coffee.

"What did you just say?"

"Within the last couple of hours we've arrested six of your criminal associates at your cabin in White Plains. It seems they were holding a certain secretary hostage. With some help from a close friend of Sonny Thomas, they are now under the jurisdiction of the Federal government. We also within the last hour have arrested 25 of your key personnel from your business world. They were taken before they could even change."

C.J. Jeffers just heard heavy breathing on the other end of the phone. He patiently waited for a response from Alexander Martinorelli. He stood up and walked toward his window.

"You have to answer for the murders and the kidnapping Mr. Martinorelli. You are responsible for those crimes in an effort to get your discs back from your daughter-in-law. "

Alexander Martinorelli said nothing. He walked to his living room and looked into his spacious backyard. He did not know how long it would remain his. Alexander was speechless.

"Are you ready to come in and talk to us?"

"Special Agent Jeffers, I am a lawyer and businessman. I have no idea what you are talking about regarding a kidnapping or murders. Sure, I will come in and talk. Give me an hour or so."

"Can't wait."

Ninety minutes later, Alexander Martinorelli walked into the New York City FBI headquarters accompanied with his personal attorney, Charles Stefano, New York Court of Appeals Judge, Alfred Rossi and the temporary New York Police Chief, Joseph Massaro.

The four men were lead into the conference room. They sat and were given coffee and water as they waited. Special Agent C.J. Jeffers walked into the conference room. He sat directly across from Alexander Martinorelli and half smiled at him.

"Thank you gentlemen for coming at such short notice. I felt it was time we met. Since the disappearance of Stephanie Martinorelli there have been 2 murders and 1 kidnapping."

"Special Agent Jeffers, initially I advised my client not to cooperate with the FBI without a warrant. Mr. Martinorelli simply refused my professional advice, saying that he is willing to assist the FBI in any way he is able."

"I appreciate your client's loyalty to the FBI. The reason we asked Alexander here, was to answer direct questions regarding the whereabouts of his daughter-in-law, Stephanie Martinorelli; the death of Police Chief, Rodger Fordrani; the death of Louis Charles, and his responsibility for the kidnapping of Sonny Thomas' secretary. Before I finish, as I indicated on the phone, Ashley is safe and sound. She was rescued at your cabin, Alexander. Six of your associates have been arrested. What a coincidence, huh?"

The four men did not say a word. In fact, they seemed disinterested about the entire matter. Stefano whispered in the ear of his client who nodded and looked straight through Special Agent Jeffers. After a few moments of silence C. J. Jeffers rose from his seat. He was directly across from Alexander staring back at him. He looked at Stefano and addressed him.

"We here at the FBI, Mr. Stefano, feel that your client is responsible for all of these crimes in the last few days. All these crimes emanated subsequent to Stephanie Martinorelli's disappearance with the discs that we know will incriminate your client to several authorities. We are certain that when we receive these discs your client will be headed to federal prison. We are very close to receiving them as we speak."

Alexander Martinorelli stood up, poured himself a glass of water and drank all of it. He stood up tightened his tie and began to circle the conference table as he spoke.

"Special Agent Jeffers, it's true that Stephanie is on the run with that character, Sonny Thomas, but that is between husband and wife. A marital discord, that is all. As for the murders of the Police Chief Fordrani the media seems to point the finger at Sonny and Stephanie, not me. I know nothing about the DA's murder or the kidnapping. That is all I know. I have a clean record. If there is anything that I can do to assist you, feel free to contact my office."

C.J. Jeffers stood up and walked toward Alexander who was now seated and seemingly content with his statements to the Special Agent. Jeffers was getting angry and rolled up his white sleeves of his dress shirt. He stood next to Alexander and raised his voice.

"Mr. Martinorelli, your daughter-in-law is on the run because she has in her possession the discs that will ruin you. You know it, and that is why you are making mistake after mistake trying to find them. The secretary was rescued at your cabin. You can act innocent and smug now, but we will get the discs first and then you will be where you belong. Federal prison."

Alexander Martinorelli did everything that he could to control his temper after listening to the truth. He then stood up face to face with Special Agent Jeffers.

"Do you have any other questions? My time is valuable, I must go. One thing before I go Special Agent Jeffers. I want you to check the last four decades of my life. Examine the United States Presidents and Senators that I have been on a first name basis with.

Investigate how my foundations have fed and assisted people all over the United States and Europe. After this Special Agent Jeffers, ask yourself what you personally have done even remotely compared to what I have done to better society in such an altruistic manner. Nothing is what you have done other than incriminate innocent charitable individuals like myself. "

He then stood up triumphantly and walked slowly out of the conference room with his small entourage. The three gentlemen followed him out the conference door. Before he opened the door, C. J Jeffers raised his voice an octave higher and yelled:

"You're going down Mr. Martinorelli. I don't care who you know, or what you've done. You can't murder innocent people to get what you want. I am going to get you. Funny that you've never mentioned the *Commission* that you have been a member of for over forty years. How come? Because if I don't get you, they will."

Alexander Martinorelli never slowed down or turned around, but he knew everything Jeffers just said was the truth. He squeezed his two hands together making fists of both of them.

Thirty Two

Petey Mancini and Michael Martinorelli just passed through the New York State toll booths just outside of Buffalo, New York. Mancini was anxious to find Sonny Thomas and Stephanie Martinorelli. He was perfectly fine with being an associate of Alexander Martinorelli in the legitimate world. Michael woke from a light sleep. He rubbed his eyes.

> "Petey, we have to check in with the local chapter and see if there is anything further on Sonny and Stephanie. I am starving. I heard their Italian food is delicious."
>
> "Sounds good Boss. We should be there within a half an hour."

Although it was early morning, the three sat in the restaurant and ate peppers and sausage, linguine, salad and even drank some red wine. The famous restaurant was located on West Ferry Street in Buffalo, New York. They were world famous for their food. The inside of the restaurant was inundated with pictures of various Italian actors, singers and any celebrity of Italian descent. The associate discussed various strategies to find anyone in Western New York. Michael and Petey listened intently.

There were no updates regarding the whereabouts of Sonny and Stephanie. The local Buffalo Police Department was advised of the fact that two murder suspects may be loose in Western New York. Afterwards, there were handshakes then Petey and Michael left the restaurant and headed north.

"Huntington, anything else on the whereabouts of Sonny and Stephanie?"

"Sir, the last sighting was Dansville, New York."

"We have a Federal building in Rochester and Buffalo. Didn't Sonny's background indicate that he is originally from Western New York?"

"It did, Sir."

"Let's get a flight to Buffalo as soon as we can. I have a hunch."

"On it, sir."

As C.J. Jeffers sat in the Federal Jet waiting to take off, he day dreamed about the opportunity of putting Alexander Martinorelli away. He thought about his Law School days and while he loved the theory of law he did not care for the practice of law once he graduated. He decided to apply to the FBI. Since Quantico, he excelled in every field assignment except the two times that he was assigned surveillance on Alexander Martinorelli a couple of years ago. They were unable to obtain any evidence of any illicit activity whatsoever. It exasperated Jeffers that the old man escaped any indictments. He now thought he knew how he had done it.

"Huntington, any news on the mole inside of the Bureau yet?"

"As a matter of fact sir, Special Agent Damian Parker is in custody and being interrogated as we speak. His bank account did not reflect his earnings of the last ten years. He also had viable access to be a third party on any line in the New York Office."

"Good. Let me know the final result."

Thirty Three

She watched the news the past forty-eight hours and was pleasantly surprised that Alexander Martinorelli's picture was on the television repeatedly. She knew that certainly was not his choice. For over forty years, Mary Fabruguzzio could do nothing to avenge the assassination of her husband, Pete Fabruguzzio, at the hands of Alexander Martinorelli. For over forty years she knew who the killer was. She was a young wife of a powerful man 30 years her senior; but, she would always be supported financially by Martinorelli. Her two young children, at the time, had all of their school and college completely paid for by Martinorelli or some corporation that he owned. She did fine financially; however, she was then twenty eight years old. She really never had a choice to avenge the death of her husband. She worried about the safety of her children, if she ever considered testifying against Martinorelli. She was 68 years old and her health was failing. She knitted her sweater contemplating what to do. She could not concentrate and put her needles down.

She was almost certain that she was the only eyewitness to the murder of her husband other than the active participants. Wouldn't now be an ideal time to talk to someone and explain what she witnessed all those years ago. She knew nothing of the law. Maybe, her coming forward would assist in destroying Alexander Martinorelli once and for all. She walked around her living room now in tears. She picked up the phone and dialed.

Thirty Four

Alexander Martinorelli paced back and forth at his office. The morning visit at FBI headquarters had him concerned. C.J. Jeffers knew about the discs. The FBI was getting close to getting the discs according to the Special Agent. Over 30 of his people had been arrested and Thomas' secretary was rescued. Heads were going to roll for that he thought. He fixed himself another cup of coffee. He sat in his leather chair and daydreamed about the old days before he was made "Boss", then his cell phone rang,

"Pop, it's me Michael."

"Any good news, Michael?"

"We think they are somewhere near or in Western New York. We have over a hundred bulls trying to find them."

"You understand that if we do not get those discs before they turn them over to the FBI we are finished."

"I do pop. Salvatore is somewhere close, also. He always finishes the job. The local police are all taken care of. The local associates are all on board assisting as much as possible."

"Let me know when the job is done, not a second before."

"I will, pop."

Alexander Martinorelli hung up the phone. If they get those discs to the FBI the *Commission* would turn their back on him. He was certain of it. He dialed his cell,

"Stefano here, how can I help you Alex?"

"Please meet me at my office. I must speak with you about something you mentioned yesterday."

"On my way, Alex. See you in about an hour."

Charles Stefano walked into the office and closed the door approximately one hour later. He sat down. He opened his briefcase and pulled out his files. He rummaged through them.

"You want some coffee?"

"Sure."

"Charley, with all of the press and internet coverage, I am beginning to think that I made a few hasty, less than intelligent decisions. I should have been more patient, but *those discs mean everything*. There is no gray area here. If the FBI gets those discs I am history as are all my business associates on those discs. Let me ask you this, what happens if the FBI gets the discs and the *Commission* starts their own investigation into this matter?"

"I've already worked on that. Were the discs to be handed over to the FBI, we allege evidentiary issues such as whether the evidence was in the proper chain of custody at the time that it was taken, which was larceny; and, whether the discs handed to the FBI are in fact "original" and not manufactured one's. We would argue our case on the Federal Rules of Evidence. The FBI would have to prove that they had the original discs and not discs that were altered. It would be your word against theirs. What are their names, Stephanie and Sonny. Alex you'll win. You have the power and have the money to fight the FBI indefinitely."

"I like that strategy. What about my associate's at the *Commission*?"

"The only thing we can do is plead your innocence and argue that the discs are not yours. You or anyone in your family would never put the *original discs* in a position that anyone could take possession of them. We will argue that the discs that Sonny and Stephanie have are in fact a fraudulent misrepresentation of your businesses all over the country. Every foundation you own will be brought up. Every donation over the last forty plus years will be brought up. It will be a public relations nightmare for the FBI."

"OK, that seems like a sound strategy. I wish that secretary was not able to escape. I want the names of the two associates who had the responsibility of keeping her in our possession. Make that first on your agenda. That must be dealt with immediately. Have Rocco deal with them ASAP. They were his men. Well, I feel a little better."

"Hold on Alex. You're not out of the woods yet."

"What. What do you mean?"

"Roger Fordrani, Louis Charles and the kidnapping of Thomas' secretary were your direct orders. You never had any type of buffer. In your desperation you reacted badly in my opinion."

"Each of these crimes portrays a nexus to Sonny Thomas and Stephanie Martinorelli."

Alexander Martinorelli knew his attorney was correct. He was not himself the last seventy-two hours. He was desperate. Tony Elia, Petey Mancini, and his own son Michael Martinorelli could turn on the old man any minute. His brief period of feeling better ended abruptly.

"Other than the last couple of days, are there any other crimes that you were directly or indirectly involved with that could come back to haunt you? You have to be one-hundred percent honest with me. If there are I have to know. I have to know how to protect you if there was any other crime. "

Alexander Martinorelli closed his eyes and thought of the murder of his mentor, Pete Fabruguzzio. He now felt sick to his stomach. He had to tell his personal Attorney that he murdered Pete Fabruguzzio all those years ago.

" Charley, I have to tell you something."

Thirty Five

In the presence of her attorney, Mary Fabruguzzio explained being a witness to the murder of her husband, Pete Fabruguzzio, forty plus years earlier at the hands of Alexander Martinorelli. Rob Muir sat back at his desk and digested the ramifications that this witness coming forward could do to the reign of Alexander Martinorelli and his organization. He just sat behind his desk and took down some notes.

"Mary, you do understand that he will come after you with everything that he has, don't you?"

"I do. I am ashamed that I did not come forward earlier. He always seemed impenetrable. Now with this Sonny and Stephanie circus that is going on he seems weak. There are murders happening and kidnapping and they all have ties to Alexander. Maybe this will help out Stephanie and Sonny. Alexander is a cold blooded murderer. I demand justice for my late husband. "

She steadily cried. She grabbed the bottle of water her attorney brought her.

"Your testimony against Alexander will put him in Federal Prison. There is no Statute of Limitations on

Murder. As long as you make it to trial and tell the jury what you just told me, he'll be found guilty. You are a very brave woman to do this, Mary. I have the utmost respect for you."

She nodded and seemed determined that her mind was made up. She looked at Rob Muir and sort of smiled. It was a smile that contained a lot of regret and past sorrow. She wished she could have done this earlier in her life, but maybe now her coming forward would rid this murderer of his pleasant, lucrative life and hopefully put an end to it. She smiled, again.

"I will have to make arrangements for you to be placed into the Witness Protection program. You may want to speak to your children and grandchildren about your final decision."

"My children were so young when it happened. How can anyone erase a father as easy as Alexander did? For power. For money. I should have come out with the truth immediately. I should never have permitted that bastard to take over for my husband."

Mary cried and grabbed a handkerchief. She stood up triumphantly and stood directly across from her attorney.

"If I don't act now I will never be able to look at myself in the mirror again. I know he never saw me that night. I knew how much power Pete had and that his death was part of the life that he chose. That murderer never thought of Pete's family. He never thought how not having a father affected his children. He never thought about a twenty-eight year old widow who would never marry again. He only thought of himself and his ascension into power because of his then bosses murder."

Rob Muir made a few telephone calls. He looked at his client and his heart broke for her. How can anyone live with what she has endured for a lifetime? With all the power that Alexander Martinorelli has this would not be easy for his client or for that matter his firm and his own personal life. He was up for the challenge he thought.

"I want to avenge the murder of Pete Fabruguzzio, my husband, and father of my children. I want to be able to look myself in the mirror again."

Thirty Six

Stephanie lay next to him and just looked at the closed eyes of Sonny Thomas. Even though they were on *the run* from just about everyone, she felt safe and at peace with Sonny at her side. She made a mistake by not leaving Michael and staying with Sonny after they graduated from Law School. You don't cry for a week when you make the *right* decision. The marriage to Michael was over almost after it began. Today they would get the discs to the FBI and begin their new life together.

She showered and dressed quickly and wanted to surprise Sonny with some breakfast. In her excitement, she forgot his specific instructions never to leave his side, even for a minute. They were in Orchard Park, New York. They were far enough away from her father-in law she thought.

Stephanie started the vehicle and felt a cold steel object press very hard at the base of her neck. She froze with terror. It had to be one of Alexander's bulls.

"Drive across the street and pull into that vacant lot. None of the stores are open yet. I need you to get Mr. Martinorelli's discs for me. "

Stephanie did as she was told. She tried to maintain her composure. She did not utter one word. She knew she was going to die. The guy with the pistol at the base of her neck did not seem pleased. Why didn't she listen to Sonny.

"I need the discs ma'am. Where are they?"

"You can have them, they are in our motel room."

Salvatore grinned. He pulled the trigger back, pressing the gun even harder at the base of her neck. Tears fell on her cheeks.

"Call him. Now!"

At the direction of Salvatore, Stephanie drove back across the street and parked in front of their motel room. He dialed Sonny's phone number. There was an answer.

"Hello, who is this?"

Sonny immediately noticed that Stephanie was not in bed with him. He checked the entire room. She was gone. He listened.

"Look out the window, Thomas."

Sonny opened the curtains. He observed Stephanie in the driver seat with a man directly behind her holding a gun to the back of her neck. He told her never to leave his side. He was both angry at her and scared for her life simultaneously.

"Bring the discs to room twenty-four directly across from you. No funny business either Mr. Thomas, or you won't want what's left of your girlfriend. You have one minute."

"Let me throw some pants on. Do not touch a hair on her head. I'll bring the discs right over."

"Again, you have one minute or I start cutting parts off of her."

He had an idea. The only thing he could think of. Sonny dressed and walked over with the original discs and the three copies. He realized that the probability of Stephanie and him remaining alive now was remote. He hoped that his quick plan would work. It was their only chance. Why did she leave his side? He could not think of that now. Sonny knocked on the door. Salvatore opened the door and smiled eerily at Sonny.

"Put the discs on the bed. I have to frisk you. You didn't think you were going to get away with stealing from the Boss did you?"

After the pat down Salvatore walked over and examined the discs.

"See that was not hard was it, Mr. private investigator. What kind of private investigator are you anyway? I found you two in Batavia in the middle of the night. I was just waiting for a mistake, which did not take long at all."

"Where is Stephanie?"

Salvatore walked to the bathroom and came out with his forty-five at the head of a tied up Stephanie. Tears were gently flowing on her cheeks when she saw Sonny. He shook his head at her.

"Put the first disc into the laptop."

Sonny did as he was told. Salvatore was satisfied. Suddenly, there was a knock on the door. Salvatore glared at Sonny.

"Sir, the ice that you ordered is here."

Salvatore continued to glare at Sonny. He walked past Sonny and began to open the door while pointing the gun at Sonny's head. At that instant, Sonny grabbed the right arm of Salvatore and a shot was fired re-actively. He kicked Sonny in the groin knocking him to his knees. Salvatore lunged at Sonny, but Sonny drop kicked Salvatore knocking him into the wall.

Stephanie, still tied up, tried desperately to get loose. She was terrified and screamed Sonny's name.

" Sonny!"

The motel manager ran back to his office.

Sonny and Salvatore exchanged an endless amount of punches to the each others head and body. As the two broke apart, Salvatore reached for his knife and sliced the right pectoral muscle of Sonny. He dropped to his knees again.

Salvatore went to stab Sonny again when Sonny lunged for the forty-five that was now under the twin bed. Salvatore repeatedly kicked Sonny in the ribs. Sonny was getting light headed. He could not reach the forty-five and Salvatore sliced the left bicep of Sonny. He screamed in pain. Stephanie was crying profusely now. She could not untie herself.

Sonny, finally, grabbed the forty-five and while on the ground next to the bed turned and faced Salvatore. Salvatore lunged in the air directly toward Sonny, his knife aimed square at Sonny's heart. Sonny fired the forty-five three times at Salvatore in mid-air. Stephanie screamed.

Thirty-Seven

"Are you OK, Sonny?"

"I've definitely been better."

"I need some first aid as quickly as you can get it."

Sonny untied Stephanie who hugged him still crying. He instructed her what he needed. She ran down the motel manager who had brought the ice to room twenty-four. She was able to calm him down. Luckily, the motel had medical supplies. She came back with a first aid box.

Salvatore Puzero laid dead on the floor. Sonny's first shot was lethal, the other two were just in case. Sonny feared the worst was not over. Stephanie washed the two wounds with soap and water. Then she rubbed some rubbing alcohol over them. Sonny winced on more than one occasion. She then taped the gauze around Sonny's chest and back and did the same for his left bicep.

"I think he might have broken my ribs. That was a close call. We have to get these original discs to the FBI today. Time is running out on us."

Stephanie gave him some Ibuprofen 800. She helped Sonny to the vehicle. He was in rough shape. She returned with the discs and their suitcases.

"We have to go, Stephanie. I feel alright. We don't have a choice we have to move."

"Sonny, call the FBI before we run out of time."

"I will. I have to figure out where I should put the original discs first. Let's head toward Goat Island in Niagara Falls, New York. I think I have the perfect spot to put the original discs."

Stephanie drove and the tires squealed out of the motel parking lot. She headed north towards Niagara Falls as per Sonny's direction. Police sirens were heard in the background as she drove through a couple of side streets away from the motel.

"Steph, when you see a parking lot pull over. It's time I called Special Agent, C.J Jeffers."

"OK. Feeling any better?"

"Once the Ibuprofen kicks in I will be alright."

Stephanie made a right and proceeded down the street. Sonny was still in a significant amount of pain. He pulled out his Smart Phone.

"There is a park and softball diamond. Pull over, Steph."

Sonny got out of the vehicle and sat at a picnic table. Stephanie followed him. Sonny dialed the number on his cell.

"This is Special Agent Jeffers, how can I help you?"

"This is Sonny Thomas. My buddy Lou Charles told me to call you. He said you were on my side. Is that correct, sir?"

"Thomas, what took you so long? I want Martinorelli as bad as you two do. Where are you guys?"

Sonny felt relieved as he sensed that Lou was right about Jeffers.

"We are in Orchard Park, New York a suburb of Buffalo, New York. The last couple of days have been crazy. I think you know the story. My secretary was kidnapped and Lou was murdered. We are alleged to have murdered a Police Chief. We are still on the run."

"Sonny, I'm happy to report to you that Ashley was rescued last night. Well, I should say that Lisa Taylor rescued her. Are you OK, Sonny?"

Sonny told Stephanie that Ashley was OK. She grabbed her mouth and tears fell from her eyes. Sonny grabbed Stephanie and kissed her on her wet cheek.

"Thank God, I was very worried that Martinorelli was going to murder her also. I just killed one of Martinorelli bulls in self-defense at the Orchard Park Motel. I had to do it, he stabbed me twice and I think he broke a few of my ribs. Special Agent, I've never killed anyone in my life. "

"Thomas, are you OK? You sound a little weak."

"I'll be OK. I have to get the discs to you today. I have the original discs which is paramount because of the evidentiary issues. We must have the original to properly indict Martinorelli. I made copies to stall anyone who is chasing us until you have the original discs."

"I just landed in Buffalo twenty minutes ago. Where do you want to meet?"

"Not yet. I can't take a chance. His men have been on our tails for a few days now. There is no telling where the next bull will pop up."

"Sonny, what do you want me to do?"

"Meet me in Niagara Falls, Ontario, in two hours at the local police agency headquarters. If I can get over the border, I will have sufficient time to place the discs at a secure location away from Martinorelli's men. His associate's probably do not have viable passports or even an enhanced driver's license. That should delay them at customs. By then I will have hid the original **Twelve Discs** at a location only you and I will know.

"I am impressed, Sonny. No wonder the old man can't find you."

"Special Agent Jeffers, Stephanie means the world to me and we are madly in love with each other. Please help us, sir."

"I will see you then."

"Sonny, if something happens before then call or text me on my cell. We are too close not to get Alexander. You have done an excellent job."

"Thanks, I have to go. I will text you the exact location of the original **Twelve Discs**."

Thirty Eight

The FBI special agents out of Buffalo, New York arrived at the Orchard Park motel within twenty minutes subsequent to the conversation between C.J. Jeffers and Sonny Thomas. The New York City Special Agents C.J. Jeffers and Evan Huntington pulled into the motel. One of the FBI special agents out of Buffalo was taking a statement from the hotel manager.

"Sonny Thomas just gave me an idea about what happened here. It appears to be another button man of Martinorelli. Sonny admitted he was responsible, but it was self-defense according to him. We have to meet with them before Martinorelli. His luck can't last forever. He sounded like he was in a lot of pain. He will get the original discs to us today."

C.J. Jeffers cell phone rang. He looked at the number.

"This is special agent Jeffers, how can I help you?"

"Hi sir, it's Lisa Taylor."

"Are you OK? Excellent job last night, even though you disobeyed my direct order."

"Sorry, I don't work for the FBI. I am about an hour out of Buffalo traveling westbound on the I-90. What can I do to help you guys with Sonny?"

C.J. Jeffers thought about it. She is a private investigator and a former cop. She somehow out smarted two assassins last night and saved the life of Ashley. He decided.

"Meet me at a Tim's coffee shop around the 5000 block area on Main Street, Williamsvile, New York. It is located within minutes once you drive through the toll booths. It's right there when you get off on the second Main Street exit. I have a way you can help Sonny."

"I will see you then."

After he hung up with Lisa Taylor, another thought entered his mind. Stephanie does have an identical twin sister. Why not get her here? She also can assist her sister at her time of need.

"Huntington, get Sarah Dempsey, Stephanie's identical twin, on a Federal Jet to Buffalo, New York as soon as possible. She may be able to help her sister now."

Within an hour Special Agent C.J. Jeffers met up with Lisa Taylor and he explained his plan to her over a late breakfast and a few cups of coffee. Within ninety minutes Sarah Dempsey walked into the coffee shop accompanied by Special Agent, Evan Huntington. C. J. Jeffers reiterated his plan to Sarah and Evan. After some deliberation back and forth they all parted and headed to Niagara Falls, Ontario where this chase after Sonny and Stephanie would hopefully end.

C.J. Jeffers cell phone rang. He glanced at the caller ID.

"This is Special Agent Jeffers, how can I help you?"

C.J Jeffers smiled. He made a fist of both of his hands and shook them.

"Really? I knew they would find something. OK, get the arrest warrant completed and call me back. I want him picked up ASAP. We can't make any mistakes with this guy."

"Who was that, sir?"

"Huntington, a witness has come forward and is allegedly an eyewitness to the murder of Pete Fabruguzzio a long time ago."

"OK , I don't get it. How is that relevant to us?"

"The eyewitness was the wife of Pete Fabruguzzio. The murderer was none other than Alexander Martinorelli."

Thirty Nine

Tony Elia looked at the floor after telling Alexander that Salvatore Puzero was dead. It was most likely at the hands of Sonny Thomas. The old man remained abnormally silent for what appeared to be an eternity. He remained sitting and stared at his most prized pictures on the wall behind his desk. After some time he said,

"Get Michael on the phone."

"Yeah, what's up pop?"

"Pop nothing. Salvatore Puzero is dead. We must get those two today. It's about time you did something to eradicate what you let your wife get away with. You are a disgrace to the Martinorelli name. Do something about it."

Stephanie drove Northbound headed for Niagara Falls, New York. Then they would cross the Rainbow Bridge into Niagara Falls, Ontario. Sonny tried to rest, but he was still in a lot of pain. As they crossed over the North Grand Island Bridge, Sonny told Stephanie to go to Goat Island. It was a little Island that separated Niagara Falls and its sister falls commonly referred to as the Whirlpool Falls. Niagara Falls, one of the wonders of the world, was located in the United States. The Whirlpool Falls was located in Ontario, Canada. Stephanie drove to a secluded part of Goat Island. This part of the island was covered with trees and vacant land.

"Pull over there Steph. Stay here. Lock the doors and keep those sunglasses and hat on. I will be right back."

Sonny went into the trunk and grabbed a small shovel. He already had the original **Twelve Discs**. He jogged deep into the woods alone.

Stephanie waited in the vehicle. She thought to herself, *was this thing ready to be over.* Sonny really should be in a hospital with those stab wounds, not running from everyone. She knew the Rainbow Bridge was close. Niagara Falls roared in the background. The Rainbow bridge was within walking distance. As soon as they passed through customs on the Canadian side, they would finally be done with this nightmare.

Sonny came jogging back and put the small shovel back into the trunk. He walked around to the drivers side. He texted Jeffers the exact location of the *Twelve Original Discs*. His job was complete. They had won. Alexander Martinorelli was finished. He smiled.

"Steph, I'm OK to drive."

The two exchanged seats and headed toward the Rainbow bridge. Once on the bridge, Sonny knew his plan had worked. It was close to 1:00 pm. He passed through customs on the United States side, and was now behind a bridge full of vehicles heading to Ontario, Canada. All that stopped them was a traffic jam.

Forty

Lisa Taylor and Sarah Dempsey talked nonstop from Buffalo to the Peace Bridge, a bridge that connected Buffalo, New York of the United States to Fort Erie, Canada. The bridge was half full, but the line went fast. The two special agents in the front seat never said a word. Lisa was extremely tired as she drove all night to get here to help Sonny. The coffee was a life saver. Sarah was happy to be able to assist her twin sister.

"Lisa, you must be exhausted after driving all night."

"I am, but I feel I have to be there for Sonny. This Martinorelli guy is very powerful and very dangerous. Luckily they both are OK. It could not have been easy for them."

"If what Special Agent Jeffers told us is accurate, this will be over shortly."

" I certainly hope so."

Charles Stefano looked pale as he entered the office of Alexander Martinorelli. He went and poured himself a shot of Anisette.

"What's wrong, Charley?"

"Alex, the FBI is on their way over to arrest you for the murder of Pete Fabruguzzio in 1975. They allegedly have an eyewitness, his wife, Mary Fabruguzzio. She just came forward, probably because of this Sonny and Stephanie thing."

"Charley, that was over forty years ago."

"Alex, it doesn't matter, there are not any statute of limitations on murder."

"How can this be? I was alone. I am positive there was nobody around. There were no witnesses!"

"Alex, you're already admitted to me that you did it."

"Attorney-Client privilege."

"Look, apparently, Mary Fabruguzzio is in failing health. She has nothing to lose. All of this business with Sonny Thomas and Stephanie, she must have felt that you have become susceptible and weak. I'm sorry Alex."

"Where should I go? I have never been on the run from anything. Ever."

"Initially, like we discussed, I think you should go to Toronto, Canada, you have property there, relax, hang out. If the situation is still the same then go to Europe for at least a year. If the witness dies, which is a distinct possibility, your case will be dropped. Plus, we have the argument over the authenticity of the discs. I will figure a way to stall this as long as you need. Right now you have to run. Disappear now."

"That Sonny Thomas, I swear, I will not rest until he is dead. Stephanie could never have done this without his assistance. Michael will have to answer for this, blood or not."

"Alex, I understand, but you don't have that luxury now. Hurry up and pack. The FBI is on their way over here. They could knock on this door any second."

"OK, OK , I am not used to being told what to do."

Within minutes, Alexander Martinorelli was on the run...*for the rest of his life.*

Forty One

Sonny texted to Special Agent C.J. Jeffers the exact location of the *original discs.* This matter was going to be over. Finally. He looked at Stephanie, who was just as exhausted as he was. Hopefully, the FBI will be on the other side of the Rainbow Bridge.

"I can't believe this line, Steph."

"I know, but that casino over there does pretty good and a lot of their customers come from the United States. The place you hid the original discs is it safe?"

"I think so. Soon the FBI will have possession of the original discs. I wish he would text me and tell me he had them. Guess I am a little anxious. Don't worry, once we are on the other side of this bridge this nightmare will be over. Alexander Martinorelli days of being a free man will be over."

"We have to get you to a hospital right away you are getting more pale by the second."

"I can last a little while longer."

Petey Mancini drove well in excess of the speed limit as he approached Niagara Falls, New York. Michael Martinorelli appeared not himself, and not very happy at the moment.

"Petey, where would they go?"

"Not sure, boss."

"Do you think they would try to leave the country and go to Canada to leave the United States jurisdiction and stall for more time? Let me make some phone calls and see if any of our associates saw them. I have to prevent Stephanie from getting those discs to the FBI or I am history."

C.J. Jeffers and Evan Huntington said nothing as they drove over the North Grand Island Bridge destination – First, Goat Island to pick up the original discs, then to Niagara Falls, Ontario to meet up with Sonny and Stephanie. The last few days have been very stressful at the Bureau. They both wanted this to be over. Then C.J Jeffers spoke,

"You know Huntington, when we get the original discs from Sonny and Stephanie, Alexander Martinorelli will go down. The discs along with the murder of the former head of the family will certainly cast him in a different light with the *Commission*. They certainly will not appreciate the fact that Alexander did not take care of this criminal act and the discs properly. I understand not realizing your murder of the former head of the family had an eyewitness, but a person in that position of authority should have investigated with certainty whether or not the murder was witnessed. He will fall on his own carelessness and negligence. He has no one to blame but himself. He was and is a very corrupt individual. Now he will pay the price."

"Corruption breeds corruption, right sir?"

"Yes, but as a Federal Agent our job is to curtail it to the best of our professional ability. Being able to put someone like Alexander Martinorelli away happens once every twenty years. As long as the general public recognizes that we go after characters like Alexander

Martinorelli as our modus operandi, they will appreciate the country that they live in and what we stand for – Life, Liberty and the Pursuit of Happiness."

"What do you think sir, the ruling Board of *Commission will* do with Martinorelli?"

"Based on what I know about the *Commission*, they will remove him from their "membership" or Board of Directors. Then they will publicly deny that they ever had a relationship with him or that they had any knowledge of his criminal background. Even if we obtain the discs and the information on his business associates throughout the United States, the power that they have will make Alexander a fading memory. Still, if we were able to bring someone like Martinorelli to justice, it would make me somewhat content. The *Commission*, on the other hand, is an entirely different matter."

Forty Two

Michael Martinorelli and Petey Mancini parked their vehicle before reaching the Rainbow Bridge. The bridge was bumper to bumper all the way across to Canada. They knew it would take forever to get across the bridge.

"Petey, where could they possibly be? I called an associate, he said he would get back to me ASAP. "

"They probably are in this area trying to hook up with the FBI. Salvatore was killed outside Buffalo. That was a couple of hours ago."

Michael's cell phone rang. Michael looked at Petey.

"Hello, this is Michael Martinorelli. What do you have? "

"Sir, they were spotted on the Rainbow Bridge a short time ago. They still may be on the bridge stuck in that traffic jam."

"Are you kidding me? Tell our men to be patient and have them wait on the U.S side until they talk to me."

Michael jumped out of the car. He instructed Petey to follow him. Petey locked the car and met Michael at the side of the car.

"Petey, let's go. They were spotted on the Rainbow Bridge. We can get them by foot. Let's go!"

"This is Special Agent Jeffers, any update on the whereabouts of Sonny and Stephanie? "

FBI Special Agent Mark Russell was nervous. He just graduated from Quantico three months earlier and wanted to impress supervision. He checked the surveillance tape near the Rainbow Bridge.

"Yes, sir. The two are presently stuck in traffic on the Rainbow Bridge. They have been stuck in traffic for a little while. The traffic seems to be stopped. There must be something going on at the Canadian side."

"OK, good. Any sign of Martinorelli or any of his associates? They have to be closing in after the incident in Orchard Park earlier."

"No, not yet. Let me double check something sir. It looks like two unidentified men, one a very large man, are walking across the bridge now and they are looking into every vehicle."

" Anything else special agent?"

"Sir, it appears that the two men have guns."

"Huntington, get me to the Rainbow Bridge."

Stephanie looked at Sonny as they waited on the bridge. He was in a lot of pain, but he was trying to hide it from her. She was getting nervous that he may pass out.

"Sonny, are you OK?"

"Yeah. Glad this will be over soon?"

"Sonny, remember how you said that you loved me from the first time that you saw me?"

"Of course."

"I felt the same way. I just wanted you to know that in case something happens to us. I was as infatuated with you as you were with me. "

Sonny sat upright and stared at Stephanie. His face was quizzical. He turned to her,

"Really? Then why didn't you ever tell me or ever say yes until that final week of Law School?"

"I don't know. I really thought that you were too good to be true. I thought that you would get tired of me. As long as I had the fantasy of you, that seemed to be good enough. Now, I know that my future is with you. I am sorry I didn't just stay with you after we graduated."

Sonny got close to her and kissed her ever so soft lips. He just looked into her eyes.

"Stephanie, I am the happiest man in the world. I want to marry you and have children with you. I want to grow old with you and spend as much time together as any happily married couple could. I love you with my entire existence."

The couple just hugged and snuggled for a few minutes. The line on the Rainbow Bridge was not moving. She looked at Sonny,

"Are you sure the original discs are safe at that spot on Goat Island?"

"I made sure that the original of the **Twelve Discs** were hidden safely so that even if we do not make it, the FBI will get them. I texted Special Agent Jeffers their exact location."

"Then why keep the three copies?"

"Give us time to let the FBI arrest Martinorelli and all his bulls. The longer they chase us and the duplicates the more time the FBI has to get the original discs. Martinorelli still must think that we have the original discs. Once the FBI has possession of the originals it is over."

Stephanie turned around and saw her husband, Michael Martinorelli, behind them looking into each vehicle on the Bridge. He was only about ten vehicles behind them. Sonny caught her face drain of all color.

"Sonny, it's Michael. He will kill us."

"Hold on."

Sonny put the car in reverse and backed up slightly, then put it in drive and jumped on the accelerator. He proceeded to drive on the sidewalk of the bridge as fast as he could. Blowing his horn to warn the pedestrians who were crossing the bridge by foot.

Seeing this, Michael Martinorelli fired three shots at the fleeing vehicle. He proceeded to run after their vehicle. The cars on the bridge were honking their horns and taking pictures of the action with their Smart Phones. Petey Mancini caught up with Michael. The two men were about half way over the bridge.

Sonny continued to avoid the pedestrians on the sidewalk, honking his horn repeatedly. Some jumped onto the road to avoid Sonny. He looked behind him and saw that he had separated himself from the two men.

"It's time for plan B, Steph."

"OK."

"Now, you take the discs and run as fast as you can to the Maid of the Mist. Get a yellow jacket and just blend in with the tourists until I can get there. I'll text Jeffers the updates. The FBI should already be there."

Sonny kissed and squeezed her.

"This will be over before you know it. Get going. I love you."

"Ditto."

Stephanie exited the vehicle and started to run towards the Maid of the Mist after she went through customs. She was terrified that Sonny was not next to her. She was more terrified that her husband was this close to both of them.

Sonny drove the vehicle to the end of the pedestrian sidewalk, turned the vehicle off and proceeded to walk to customs. The Canadian Custom's Officer came outside and met Sonny.

"Sir, you cannot just leave your vehicle there like that."

"I have two gentlemen chasing me on this bridge. They are trying to kill me. Look!"

The custom's officer, armed, started to walk toward the oncoming Michael Martinorelli and Petey Mancini. The two men did not slow down.

"Sir, you remain here. I will take care of this situation."

The officer saw the handguns both of the men had on them as they slowed down to walk. Several other customs officers started to get out of their offices and walk outside. The initial officer who approached the situation pulled out his gun and pointed it at the two men. Niagara Falls roared in the background and the horns of cars continued on beeping their horns partly because of the traffic jam, and partly because of what they were witnessing.

"Drop your weapons gentlemen. I am ordering you under the authority of Canadian Customs to stop and drop your weapons immediately. "

Neither man dropped their weapons. Petey just smiled. The Customs officer approached the two men that suddenly stopped. The horns of the vehicles on the bridge continued to mix in with the roar of Niagara Falls. It was deafening.

Suddenly, Michael raised his thirty-eight and shot the customs officer in his left arm. Another officer came running after hearing the gun shot and fired his gun at Petey Mancini. Mancini was shot in the chest and he dropped to his knees. The balance of custom officials ran to the scene.

Stephanie arrived at the Maid of the Mist and purchased a ticket. She was handed a yellow raincoat. She blended in nicely with the other fifty or so tourists. The roar of the Falls was all she could hear in the background. She turned and looked to see if she saw Sonny on his way. Nothing. *C'mon Sonny.* She thought. *Please hurry...*

Suddenly, someone tapped her on the shoulder. She turned around nervously.

"Sarah? What, how, what are you doing here?"

The two twins hugged each other tightly. They both wiped tears from the others cheek. Sarah turned toward someone.

"First, Stephanie I would like to introduce you to Lisa Taylor."

The two women shook hands, both eyeing each other from head to toe. They both could not believe how beautiful the other one was. Stephanie knew all about Lisa and Sonny's past. She was impressed that she was able to rescue Ashley almost by herself. Lisa was more than jealous, but appreciated how brave a thing Stephanie did to run from such a man as Alexander Martinorelli. Stephanie was the girl in his past he never would speak of. It all made sense now. She was sad.

"Well, anyway, Sarah, why are you two here, again?"

"Special Agent Jeffers had me flown into Buffalo a few hours ago. Lisa was already here. She drove all night from New York City to come and help you guys. Special Agent Jeffers has a plan to keep Martinorelli's bulls away from us until he has the original discs. He wants us to stay as close together until we have to make a run for it."

"Stephanie and Sarah, please stay close to me. If for some reason Sonny doesn't get here first and it's Michael, we have to confuse him and slow him down. We have to let him think we have the original discs. With all the confusion of the last couple of days he won't know the difference."

The three women discussed exactly what they would do if somehow Michael got to them first. They were all about the same height. They blended into the crowd, all three looking back occasionally to see if anyone was coming after them. Twenty yards away the two special agents waited also, ready for if, and, or when the action would take place.

Forty Three

Sonny could not believe what he was about to see. After Michael shot the first customs officer in the shoulder, the second officer shot Petey in the chest knocking him to his knees. Suddenly, Petey stood up. The customs officer shot Petey again, now in his left shoulder, but Petey kept charging forward. He reached at the officer and knocked the gun out of his hand. Petey then picked him up and threw him over the side of the bridge to the gorge, several hundred feet below to a certain death.

After seeing this, Sonny broke loose from another custom's officer who ran toward Petey as the rest of the customs officer's did. They were firing shots as they all ran toward Petey. One officer took a shot at the fleeing Sonny, but missed and turned his attention to Petey. Sonny was about five blocks from the Maid of the Mist.

Petey walked toward the officers who demanded that he drop his weapon or they would shoot. Petey fired a shot with his thirty-eight and struck the heart of one of the officers, killing him instantly.

Meanwhile, with all of the attention on Petey, Michael Martinorelli snuck past everyone and started to run because he knew that Sonny was ahead of him and would lead him to Stephanie and the discs. He thought he would still save the day for his father.

The custom officers had Petey backed up against the bridge. He could not go anywhere. All firearms pointed at him. Petey was stalling because he knew that this would enable Michael to get away. He would be loyal to the death he thought. His eyes teared up. He yelled and lunged toward the officers and was able to tackle two of them. The officers fired at Petey repeatedly, but he would not die.

Finally, from behind, a shot was fired and hit Petey right in between the eyes. He was dead. The shooter was Special Agent C.J. Jeffers.

Sonny was jogging toward the Maid of the Mist. He zigged and zagged around the large number of tourists. He saw the entrance for the Maid of the Mist. It was only a block away. He was almost there.

Michael Martinorelli was catching up to Sonny and reached for his thirty-eight. He stopped and fired at Sonny just nearly missing him. Sonny rolled over and landed behind a tourist souvenir shop that hid him for the moment. He was so close to the Maid of the Mist. The thunder of Niagara Falls roared in the background.

After Petey Mancini was shot by Jeffers, Evan Huntington ran up to him.

"Sir, are you OK?"

"Yeah, let's go. We have to get Sonny and Stephanie. I saw Michael Martinorelli running after him. I had to take care of this animal first."

C.J. Jeffers started to run after Michael who could not be too far ahead of him. The Maid of the Mist was reasonably close. He maintained a steady jog.

Forty Four

Alexander Martinorelli arrived at JFK airport utilizing a walker, baseball hat and huge dark sunglasses. He obviously did not did not want to be recognized. It was unknown at this point if the FBI leaked any of his eventual arrest to the internet or television. He was accompanied by his two highest members of the criminal organization, Rocco Latino and Tony Elia. Alexander approached the airport ticket counter. The two men carried all four of the suitcases.

"How can I help you, sir?"

"Yes, I would like three one-way tickets to Toronto, Canada – First Class."

The ticket agent handed the three first class tickets to the three gentlemen.

"Thank you, young man."

Alexander went through and walked through the requisite gate and sat and awaited his flight. None of the information on the identification he had on his person reflected who he really was. He was despondent. He had enough money on him to last

20 years. Credit cards that were linked to corporations he owned that would never be traced to him. He was a ghost and would remain one until this nonsense was over. He knew, however, he would win eventually. He always did.

Michael Martinorelli walked toward the Maid of the Mist. He noticed that there must be fifty tourists in yellow raincoats in the area. There was no sign of Thomas either. With his thirty-eight brandished he walked among all of the tourists. Each of the tourist's eyes opened wide when they saw the gun.

Suddenly, three of the raincoats pushed their way through the crowd. Hearing the commotion, Michael turned around and saw three women, he thought, running away from the Maid of the Mist. Then the three woman split each headed in a different direction. One ran toward the Whirlpool Falls, Southbound. The second ran directly up a steep hill, Westbound. The third ran toward the Rainbow Bridge, Northbound.

He did not know which one to follow. Thinking directly up the hill was his best chance, he ran after the yellow raincoat. He was outrunning her and eventually tackled the woman.

"Give me the discs, Stephanie."

Lisa Taylor turned over and kicked Michael Martinorelli in the groin. He screamed in pain. He pulled out his gun and pointed it right at Lisa.

"Where are Sonny and Stephanie?"

"Hey, drop that it's the FBI."

Michael turned and saw two special agents running to him with a woman next to them. He looked closer - was that Stephanie? Lisa Taylor kicked Michael in the groin again. For some reason he looked at the third yellow raincoat and she was running with a man next to her. He got up and ran toward them, limping still in some pain.

Sonny and Stephanie ran back towards the Rainbow Bridge, specifically, Clifton Hill. There were a lot of tourist attractions on this part of Niagara Falls, Ontario. Michael Martinorelli sprinted toward them.

Special Agent C.J. Jeffers arrived and Lisa Taylor and Sarah Dempsey still had their raincoats on. The two special agents told Jeffers what had happened. He looked at Lisa Taylor and just shook his head.

"Lisa, are you OK?"

"I'm OK, I am mad that he caught me so quick. I got him back though."

"Yes, you did. The two special agents told me what you did to him. I am glad you're on my side."

"Michael saw Sonny and Stephanie and he went after them. They had a generous head start though."

"What direction Lisa?"

"Clifton Hill, Northbound."

Alexander Martinorelli read the newspaper. He tried to digest what the last couple of days meant for his future. For the first time in his life, *He was on the run*. How ironic. In forty plus years, he accomplished much. He achieved power and wealth that very few people ever reach. None of that mattered now. He had lost and barring a miracle, he was done for. Alexander was unaccustomed to losing. How could his vast empire be in jeopardy because of negligence on the part of his only heir? He would still maintain that somehow he would get out of this situation. Sonny Thomas was responsible. If he did not assist Stephanie, this would have been over days ago. His murder of Pete Fabruguzzio would have remained a secret. The loud speaker announced that his plane was ready to board. He thought he would not rest until he could avenge Sonny Thomas.

Forty Five

In Newark, New Jersey members of the *Commission* met, again, regarding Alexander Martinorelli. Only the members of the east coast were present at this meeting. After greetings, the *Commission* sat down to do business. One of the Chair Members stood.

"Gentlemen, we have word that Alexander Martinorelli is on a plane, on his way to Toronto, Canada. He should have been indicted for the murder of Pete Fabruguzzio in 1975. He did not take care of business then or now. The FBI has all of the arrest warrants ready to serve him. We should meet him there, before the FBI is able to get him. We cannot take any chances on him. We cannot let him hide for the rest of his life, it is not good for the *Commission*. We handle our own, in our own way. There is nothing that we can do for him anymore. It is over."

The members of the *Commission* agreed and broke into small talk and discussions of other matters, none of which had anything to do with Alexander Martinorelli.

"Sonny, what are we going to do? Michael is right behind us."

Sonny looked at his phone. C.J. Jeffers texted him that the FBI was now in possession of the original discs of Alexander Martinorelli. He slumped his shoulders.

"Steph, the FBI has the original discs. We won! Now let's stay alive until the FBI can get here."

They both ran into a wax museum right in the middle of Clifton Hill. They paid and entered the dark museum. The museum had been there for years and every possible scary monster or thing was in it. They went all the way to the back of the museum. They spotted a Dracula wax figure. It was very dark.

"Here, Steph, hide behind Dracula. Do not move. I'll text Jeffers where we are. I'll be right back. Do NOT move. This will be over very soon."

Sonny went to the front of the museum and texted Jeffers. After he sent the text he heard a click.

"Where is she?"

Sonny could do nothing with the gun at his head. He wanted to tell Michael that it was over, but he would wait until the time was right. He walked Michael back to where Stephanie was hiding.

"Come on out Stephanie or your boyfriend is a dead man."

Stephanie came out from behind Dracula's wax figure.

"Hand them over."

Stephanie handed the three sets of duplicate discs to Michael.

"I knew I would get them. You can't outsmart a Martinorelli. Now follow me and no brave stuff Sonny or girlfriend dies. Got it."

The three walked down Clifton Hill like normal tourists. Michael had his gun in his pocket facing Stephanie which he thought was more effective because Sonny would not do anything to jeopardize her safety.

"Leave her out of this, you have the discs, you won. What else do you want?"

"It's time that you get what you deserve. It's business Mr. Thomas, nothing personal. Now let's continue to walk nice and easy so innocent bystanders do not get hurt. I don't have my passport on me so things can get ugly on this side. By the way, it was ingenious that you two chose the Canadian side. It *almost* worked."

"You'll never get away with this Michael. The FBI is here waiting for you as we speak. There are at least fifty agents here to get you."

"You don't think I know that, Thomas? That is why we are going back to the United States where I have people, including police officials, waiting for me, on the other side of this bridge."

Jeffers was watching the three walking towards the Rainbow Bridge. *I have to get closer to them,* thought Jeffers. He had an idea.

"Huntington, I need backup on both sides of the bridge, *Now.* Michael Martinorelli has both of them at gunpoint."

C.J. Jeffers ran behind the three unnoticed by Michael. He entered the cab and after a brief discussion with the cabbie, took the cabbies hat and jacket and slid into the driver's seat. The cabbie left and was soon met by two special agents.

Forty Six

The three of them stood together like normal tourists. Michael whistled for a cab. The cab quickly showed up and pulled over.

"Niagara Falls, New York. An extra hundred if we get there quick."

Special Agent Jeffers waited as the three entered the cab. Sonny sat in the back seat and Stephanie sat in the front seat with the thirty-eight held by Michael pointed directly at her.

"You know, Thomas, I have a question for you."

"What's that?"

"Did you really think you would get away with this?"

"I already have."

"What?"

"You see, you only have copies of the discs. I still have the originals. Or should I more accurately say the FBI has the original discs. They have been in possession of them since we were on the Rainbow Bridge."

"Wait a minute. You take my family's discs, my wife, and you think I won't eventually get you? My family is more powerful than any of your lawyers can ever imagine. I will decide when Stephanie leaves me. *I have the discs. In my hands, I have the discs.*"

"You have copies of the discs. The FBI has the original discs. The Martinorelli family is over. I hope you like concrete, Michael."

"You don't love me, Michael."

"No, I don't. It doesn't matter. I own you. You are my possession. I decide what to do with you. Me and me alone."

"She's going to end up with me, Michael. The FBI will have you arrested any minute. You have been chasing copies not originals. The discs that you have are meaningless. I'm sure the *Commission* will be thrilled to know that the original discs are in the hands of the FBI."

"Yeah, you're right she will end up with you. Dead."

The cab driver was trying to get Sonny's attention while he was talking with Michael. His attempts were futile, until he finally caught Sonny's attention. He managed to show his FBI badge and credentials. It was Special Agent, C.J. Jeffers. Sonny's heart jumped. He was still uncertain how they would get out of this though.

They approached the Rainbow Bridge which was congested with ambulances, helicopters, FBI agents, and both

Niagara Falls, Ontario and New York Police Agencies. Niagara Falls roared in the background.

"Sir, let me go check and see what the commotion is all about."

"Hurry up cabbie. I have important people waiting for me on the other side of this bridge."

The cabbie, C.J. Jeffers, got lost in the crowd of different police agencies. Michael waited and observed on more than one occasion that a lot of the different police officers and FBI agents were looking at the cab. Michael waited and waited. He then panicked. He left the cab with Stephanie, and began to walk briskly toward Clifton Hill.

Sonny tried to get out, but Michael had locked all of the doors in the cab somehow. C.J. Jeffers ran back into the cab.

"Sonny, where are they?"

Sonny pointed to Clifton Hill. C.J. Jeffers unlocked the doors and they both ran after Michael Martinorelli and Stephanie.

Michael pushed and pulled Stephanie up Clifton Hill. She was knocked down once, scraping her knee. His gun was sticking in her back. She felt completely helpless.

"What did your boyfriend mean saying that he had the original discs?"

"Michael, what you have has no evidentiary value. Only the original discs are valid proof of all of the licit and illicit businesses that your father's organization operates. Sonny knew this and already made arrangements to have them picked up by the FBI before we were on the bridge."

"How could you do this to me, Stephanie? I gave you everything, money, success... I tried to be a good husband, but I always thought you were better than me. The other women were never as good as you. I am sorry. "

"You never loved me, Michael. You don't sleep with other women and expect me not to know. You never were exclusive with me."

"Nor were you to me."

"Only Sonny."

"So this Sonny Thomas, he loves you?"

"Yes, and I love him."

"Too bad your romance will be so short."

"You can never defeat Sonny, Michael."

The two reached the top of Clifton Hill and then vanished down a side street. Sonny and C.J. Jeffers ran to the top of Clifton Hill. The entire area was now swarming with various police agencies. The FBI still outnumbered all of the other agencies.

Sonny spotted them. He ran as fast as he could and approached them. Michael turned just as Sonny lunged and tackled him, knocking Michael's gun to the ground. Sonny landed a solid shot to the jaw of Michael and followed that with several body shots. Michael fell back on his behind and squirmed to get to his thirty-eight. As sore as Sonny was, the adrenaline kicked in and he landed as many punches as he could.

Stephanie watched in horror as the two men fought, each landing solid punches to the head and body. Stephanie felt helpless.

C.J. Jeffers saw the two men rolling on the ground from a distance. He, again, called for backup. They were now at the top of Clifton Hill. When he heard the gun shot, Sonny Thomas dropped to his knees. Stephanie screamed.

" Sonny!"

Jeffers ran toward the two men. Michael Martinorelli looked at Stephanie, he had tears in his eyes, took the discs out of his pocket and fell over. Sonny collapsed, but was alive. Sonny had fired the thirty-eight into the heart of Michael Martinorelli. He was dead.

"Sonny!"

Stephanie ran over to Sonny and kissed him. Lisa Taylor and Sarah Dempsey ran to Sonny and Stephanie. The four of them hugged one another and cried.

"It's over, Steph…it's over."

Sonny passed out. He was not in good shape and had lost a lot of blood this day. An ambulance arrived and took him to a nearby Canadian hospital. He would need emergency medical treatment for the next twenty-four hours. He was in stable condition, but he needed round the clock attention. Stephanie, Lisa and Sarah were all at his side.

Forty Seven

The Toronto airport was buzzing as usual. The flight from New York to Toronto was short, but there were several delays on land. Alexander Martinorelli, Rocco Latino and Tony Elia walked toward the black limousine at arrivals. The driver opened the door and the three men sat in the limousine as their luggage was put in the trunk by an assistant of the limousine driver.

The limousine drove away toward a townhouse that Alexander had owned for years outside of Toronto.

"Well, at least we have made it this far. I can't wait to have all of this business taken care of by my team of lawyers, Rocco, Tony. I have lawyers from all over the country. There is no chance that Sonny Thomas can beat me, let alone stay alive for much longer."

Rocco Latino and Tony Elia never said a word. They knew where Martinorelli was headed. A significant "member" of the *Commission* gave them the details earlier that day. Unfortunately, for Alexander, the *Commission* overruled everyone, including the old man.

The limousine suddenly pulled into a vacant parking lot. It appeared that no one was around for miles. Two other limousines pulled up. The limousine driver and his associate got out of the vehicle. Alexander was confused and now scared.

"Hey, what is the meaning of this?"

"Rocco, Tony, get out and see what is going on here!"

Both men looked blankly at Martinorelli. They both opened their respective limousine door and left Alexander alone in the limousine.

Alexander turned white. After Rocco and Tony left, two men in black suits joined him in the back seat. Both directly facing him. The two men were armed with thirty-eights, pointed at him. Then another unknown individual entered the front seat and started the limousine.

"What is going on here? I demand an answer! I am a very powerful man."

"You *were* a very powerful man. The **Commission** has decided your fate, Mr. Martinorelli. You see, the last couple of days you've showed the world how weak you truly are. In addition to that you never took care of business a long time ago. The **Commission** has standards that have to be kept. You no longer are a member of the **Commission** due to your failure to maintain their level of professionalism. The **Commission** can never have any weak links. It is too much of a risk. You do not deserve to be a member of the *Commission* anymore. Nothing personal, Mr. Martinorelli, but you will have to be taken care of."

Alexander Martinorelli did not utter a word. He would not cry, although he wanted too. *All my life, and this is how it will end.* He thought to himself. *I don't deserve this.* All because of Sonny Thomas.

Alexander Martinorelli shut his eyes. Suddenly, his world went black.

Alexander Martinorelli was dead.

Forty- Eight

Sonny awoke a day later and was hooked up to an IV machine. He was in a lot of pain. Stephanie was sitting next to him, holding his hand. Special Agent C.J. Jeffers and Lisa Taylor were also in the hospital room.

"What happened?"

"You've been unconscious for the last twenty-four hours. The last couple of days were rough on your body. You'll be out in a couple of days. Relax my friend," replied Jeffers.

"Sonny, I was so worried. I love you so much," added Stephanie.

"Jeffers, I know the FBI obtained the original discs. Now what?"

"You did a great job. At the end Michael chased you like you had the originals. He never understood the evidentiary value like you and I did."

"Based on the Federal Rules of Evidence, if they were somehow able to get the originals, the copies would mean nothing. Stephanie and I just did our run and other than meeting up with a couple of Martinorelli's bulls it went, well it went, never mind. "

They all laughed. C.J. Jeffers explained that while Martinorelli landed in the Toronto airport right around the time Sonny and Michael were exchanging punches, he has not been heard of since. Sonny and C.J. Looked at each other and nodded. Jeffers pointed to Lisa Taylor.

"Sonny, this woman is incredible. She gets the address of the Martinorelli cabin, and goes there in the middle of the night. Alone. She, basically, saved Ashley herself. I'll say it again, I'm glad Lisa is on our team."

Lisa Taylor walked over to the opposite side of the bed that Stephanie was on and hugged and kissed Sonny on the cheek. She looked into his eyes like she was saying goodbye. Stephanie looked on. Her tears began to flow. She always loved Sonny and hated to let him go. She knew Stephanie was his girl from his past. She cried. She will always love him she thought, but she knew he would never be hers.

"I have to go Sonny. I was glad that I could help you guys out. You have meant the world to me. I love you, Sonny."

Lisa turned and ran out of the room crying. She was happy that she was able to help them, but she also knew that it was the end of her and Sonny. Lisa ran down the hallway her crying noticeable to everyone nearby.

"I should go too, Sonny. You two are very special people. Make sure that you contact me whenever you feel the FBI can help you at all. Your buddy, Lou Charles, what a great guy. I have to get out of here. Sonny you call me as soon as you can."

Stephanie and Sonny were alone. They obviously were in love. She went and laid next to Sonny on his hospital bed. She could not remember being this happy. She held onto him like he would vanish, if she stopped hugging him.

"Steph, I am getting sleepy. What did they give me?"

"Something that will help you get better. Don't worry, it's all good."

"Before I crash, what else can you tell me about Alexander Martinorelli?"

"Well, believe it or not, it appears that he was responsible for the death of his former Don, Pete Fabruguzzio. This happened over forty years ago. The former Don's wife, Mary, was an eyewitness to the murder. Partly because of us, she went to her lawyer and wanted to speak up and go on record as an eyewitness to the murder."

Stephanie looked at Sonny and he was sound asleep.

Forty-Nine

Six months later.

Since the disappearance of Alexander Martinorelli, there were several buyouts of companies he either owned or had a large percentage of interest in. Likewise, his real estate was sold as he did not have any living heir. His law firm had changed names, but ran it's day to day operations, never missing a beat. His criminal empire was taken over by another powerful New York family as per direction of the *Commission.*

His disappearance, obviously, removed him from being a "member" of the *Commission*, which still controls most of what goes on in strategic locations throughout the United States. His replacement on the *Commission,* an up and comer from Williamsburg, Virginia, was a solid choice. A two term former United States Senator who was formerly on the tri-lateral commission and a current member of the builderberg group.

Martinorelli would never be found, ironically, like his mentor of a lifetime ago, Pete Fabruguzzio. While he was alive, Martinorelli had it all, but his eventual indictment for the murder of his mentor only became plausible because of Sonny and Stephanie. The eyewitness would never have come forward without Stephanie getting hold of those discs.

Special Agent C.J. Jeffers did not take it too hard that Alexander Martinorelli was never found to be prosecuted for the murder of his former Don, Pete Fabruguzzio. He was fairly certain that the *Commission* took care of him.

The 1975 murder, along with the murder of Police Chief, Roger Fordrani and Assistant District Attorney, Louis Charles showed weakness and panic on the part of the old man. Tony Elia was never indicted for the murder of Fordrani.

The eyewitness, Mary Fabruguzzio, who received financial assistance from Martinorelli while she was alive, continued to receive financial assistance until the day she would die. That was justice. Her children would die millionaires because of her bravery in finally getting justice done for the death of her husband, Pete Fabruguzzio.

Jeffers and Sonny Thomas developed a friendship, along with Stephanie. They regularly spent time together. C.J. Jeffers had done his part in ridding the world of Alexander Martinorelli. His new ambition was getting a start on investigating more thoroughly the inner workings of the *Commission.* This was in his future he hoped.

Sonny was in his cloth white bathrobe on his Tablet when Stephanie walked out into the room in her silk pajamas. Sonny got up and kissed his new bride on her soft lips.

"How are you this morning, Mrs. Thomas? You look absolutely beautiful this morning. "

"A little sick to my stomach, but never better. Sonny, do you think this Martinorelli thing is really over? I still have nightmares that Michael is still alive and wants to kill us."

"I am pretty certain. I am sure that we have enemies, but, realistically, without Alexander or Michael who will pursue us? Certainly not the *Commission*. I am positive that they have already moved forward from Martinorelli. Lisa did some investigating on the *Commission* and it seems as if Martinorelli never even existed."

"Do you miss Lisa? I know what relationship you two had."

Sonny really cared for Lisa, but she was not Stephanie. It was Stephanie that was his soul mate. He loved Stephanie with all of his heart.

"No, Lisa always knew that there was someone I had in my past. She just never knew exactly who it was until she met you."

Stephanie got up and walked around the room. Sonny went back to his Tablet. Suddenly, Stephanie said,

"I have a confession to make. Remember, the last week of Law School? The couple of days and nights that we spent together?"

"Steph, how could I forget? I have been in love with you from the moment I first laid eyes on you. As your husband, I will do whatever it takes to make us as happy as possible."

"OK, I just want you to know that during that last week of Law School was the happiest time of my life. After, I wrote that note and left, I cried for a month. I imagined us growing old together, but I wanted to be pregnant so we could be together then. When I got my period, I cried even harder. I thought I would never have you. Until now."

"Steph, I do want to grow old with you."

Stephanie just smiled and looked at her stomach. Sonny's heart raced more so now than when he used to see Stephanie. He jumped up and held her close.

"What?"

"Sonny, I'm pregnant."

Sonny grabbed her and lovingly hugged and kissed her. He was absolutely the happiest he had ever been in his entire life.

"I think that I am so happy I will cry! You

never fail to amaze me, Steph."

He lovingly touched her pregnant belly. Tears flowed down Sonny's cheeks. The magical love that they had for each other had now evolved to a whole new level. The creation of something that only could be from Sonny and Stephanie. Their child.

"I love you, Stephanie Thomas."

"And, I will love you forever, Sonny."

THE END.